ADJUSTED LIVES

(STORIES OF STRUCTURAL ADJUSTMENTS)

ADJUSTED LIVES

(STORIES OF STRUCTURAL ADJUSTMENTS)

F. ODUN BALOGUN

Africa World Press, Inc.

P.O. Box 1892
Trenton, New Jersey 08607

Africa World Press, Inc.

P.O. Box 1892

Trenton, NJ 08607

Copyright © F. Odun Balogun, 1995

First Printing 1995

Book and Cover design: Jonathan Gullery

Library of Congress Cataloging-in-Publication Data

Balogun, Fidelis Odun. 1946–
     Adjusted lives : (stories of structural adjustments) F. Odun
Balogun.
          p.   cm.
     ISBN 0-86543-486-7. -- ISBN 0-86543-487-5 (pbk.)
     1. Nigeria--History--Fiction. I. Title
PR9387.9.B345A65   1995
823--dc20

                                        95-6644
                                        CIP

ACKNOWLEDGEMENTS

"The Apprentice" was first published in *Okike* 14 (September 1978) 59-63, and has subsequently appeared in anthologies and translations which include *African Short Stories,* eds. Chinua Achebe and C.L. Innes (London: Heinemann, 1985) 6-21; *African Creations,* ed. Emmanuel Obiechina (Enugu: Fourth Dimension, 1985) 128-134; *Pytonormens Dilemma: Nigerianska noveller,* trans. and ed. Mikael Dolfe (Svenska, Sweden: Askelin & Hagglund, 1986) 24-28; and *Voices From Twentieth Century Africa: Griots and Towncriers,* ed. Chinweizu (London: Faber and Faber, 1988) 232-238. *"The Gods Will Call Again"* has appeared in *Obsidian* 4.3 (Winter 1978) 55-60; *Benin Review* 2 (1980) 88-94; and *Okike* 20 (December 1981) 73-78. Part one of *"The Hyde Park Preacher"* was translated by Daniel Vignal as *"Ilu Oyinbo: La terre promise"* and published in *Europe* 618 (October 1980) 76-81. *"Mother and Son"* is published in the anthology compiled and edited by Wolfram Frommlet and titled *Contemporary African Radio Narrations* (Baden-Baden, Germany: Nomos Verlagsgesellschaft and Radio Deutsche Welle, 1992) 90-97. The story was contracted for a German translation by the same editor.

The general plot of *"Hyphenated Celebrants"* was suggested by Ayi Kwei Armah's depiction of the treacherous enslavement of the entire members of an age group of boys and girls engaged in initiation ceremonies in *Two Thousand Seasons* (Nairobi, Kenya: East African Publishing House, 1973). Also, while the general perception of the deity Ogun that operates in *"The Hyde Park Preacher"* comes in part from my reading of Wole Soyinka's works, the definition used on page 60 has been appropriated directly from a specific text—his *Myth, Literature and the African World* (Cambridge: Cambridge UP, 1976).

I owe a lot of gratitude to a number of friends and colleagues, especially Tanure Ojaide, David Dorsey and Niyi Osundare, who, in spite of busy schedules, found time to read the draft of this collection and to make helpful suggestions for improvement. I also wish to acknowledge the invaluable contributions of the following four individuals who nurtured my efforts as an apprentice writer: the Trinidadian writer and friend John Stewart who taught anthropology at the University of Illinois, Urbana-Champaign, USA, where I was a doctoral student in the 70s; Noel Pharr Davis, English professor at the same institution, who became a friend while I took his course in the short story; Viktor Andronikov Manuilov, friend and M.A supervisor at the Leningrad State University, Leningrad (St. Petersburg, Russia); and Ludmilla Kononovna Kolesova, to whom I owe my most cherished memories of Leningrad and the former Soviet Union.

I am also indebted to Emmanuel Obiechina, Chinua Achebe and Chinweizu for making the pages of Okike available to me early in my creative efforts when I most needed publishing avenues.

DEDICATION

for

The common people of Africa
Their heroes—past and present
And supporters—everywhere
In centuries of unabating battle
Against adjustments
Forever tactically packaged
In the color of the chameleon
Forever externally enforced

CONTENTS

Part One: The Philosophy

Part Two: The Heresies

Part Three: The Restoration

Part One

The Philosophy

Hyphenated Celebrants

It was evening and the sun had started its usual rapid descent, leaving the sky on the sunset side of *Ode,* a village of thrice twenty huts with a population of approximately five twenties in ten places, suffused with a translucent golden radiance. It was the dry season and the tall trees of the forest on that side of the village had cast long, mostly leafless shadows across the thatched roofs and walkways. The forest on the sunrise end was swiftly darkening with the approach of night which would reduce the waiting for the annual *Omoge* festival to only four more days.

As darkness overtook the village, the sound of pestles beating on mortars in preparation of the traditional dinner of pounded yams echoed from hut to hut. In one of the huts centrally located on the sunrise side of the square, evidently the most prosperous, the pestle was dexterously wielded by Adunke, a sixteen-year-old girl whose age group would be celebrating the *Omoge* festival in less than five days.

Adunke's father, a most successful farmer and descendant of a line of renowned warriors, was the most influential man in the village. Among his daughters, Adunke was his pride. Although she was not spectacularly beautiful, she was certainly the most sought-after of all the girls in the village, and this was not mainly because of her father's wealth. Adunke was the sort of girl who a young man, upon seeing her for the first time, immediately knew would make him happy as a wife. She was pretty in the kind of way peasants wanted their girls to be pretty: average in height, firm and strongly built, agile of limb, and with a robust body reflecting good health in the smoothness of luscious skin. These were indications that as a wife, she would be able to withstand the pressures of child-bearing and farm labor without going under prematurely. To these basic requirements, Adunke added other attractions: a winning smile and a pleasant disposition that made her company a regular pleasure to the young men who were always seeking her attention.

Anyone who saw Adunke knew immediately that she fully enjoyed the sense of being alive. She was ready to work or play as the occasion demanded. Something about her zest for life, which was moderated by a strong sense of propriety, added extra beauty to anything she did. For this reason her singing, dancing, talking, playing, walking and working had added appeal. And because she was respectful and compassionate, she was also admired by older people, for whom she was quick to render timely service. Given her reputation, it was not surprising that young men flocked to her, many of them hastily proposing marriage. With her winning ways, she always knew how to disappoint without hurting the feelings of her hasty admirers. Often she would flatter a would-be husband by saying that it was a pity he had come rather late, and that didn't he know she was already betrothed to Olusegun? After hearing this, even her most conceited suitors calmly accepted their fate, knowing they were no match for Olusegun.

Everyone, indeed, agreed that Adunke had chosen well. There was no father or mother in the village who had not secretly wished that Olusegun could be their son-in-law. He was nineteen and his father was a renowned hunter who had earned his fame by organizing the legendary hunt that had destroyed the pack of lions which had once constituted a ferocious menace, steadily decimating the village. During hunts, it was always he who devised strategies for isolating individual lions which would then be stalked and killed by the hunters. On occasion, he was said to have disappeared for days until he would suddenly reappear with the carcass of a lion he had been trailing slung on his hefty shoulders. Another peculiarity that made him famous was the fact that he ate only the meat of antelope, and he was never known to have been short of meat in his house for a single day. His wife, who had her own reputation as the priestess and custodian of the village shrine of the goddess of water and fertility, was also the most patronized of the village children's doctors. By virtue of her priesthood, she was automatically the leader of the women of the village. She fulfilled the duties of her different offices with a dignity, scrupulosity, and personal charisma that earned her the respect and love of the entire village.

Olusegun, their son, was the most eligible bachelor in the village—a position he attained almost entirely by virtue of his own reputation. Of course, it was taken for granted that to be eligible, a man or a girl had to come from a good home: hence the meticulous investigation traditionally conducted by parents and relatives into the backgrounds of a prospective son- or daughter-in-law prior to sanctioning a marriage. In the case of Olusegun, however, no such investigation was required, partly because he came from a well-known home and partly because his was already a household name. Even though, unlike his father, he had not yet performed any spectacular feat, his extant qualities exhibited so much promise that no one had any doubt that he would achieve greatness. If there was anyone in the village capable of measuring up to and even surpassing the achievements of Adunke's father, everybody knew that Olusegun was that person.

He was tall, handsome, robust, and strong. He combined an agile intellect with a pleasant, generous nature. Even in the midst of a tasking job, he had a genuine welcoming smile for everyone. He was as playful as he was hard-working. Young men of his age saw him as a natural leader and clustered around him. He was always considerate and he tried to moderate his efforts in order not to overshadow his colleagues, but he always excelled in anything he did. He haunted better, farmed better, played better, and was precociously acquiring the wisdom of proverbial speech that distinguished men of much older age. Parents always swore by his name to caution their erring sons: "You lazy stranger from my womb," a mother would address a wayward son, "are you not ashamed to show me that these are all the heaps you've cultivated all day! When last did you go to see Olusegun's barn? In case you do not know, it is still overflowing with last season's yams." Frequently too, these are the derisive words you would overhear from a father, berating a son who had returned empty-handed from a hunt: "Yes, indeed, you tried your best; you most certainly did. Yet I have learned that Olusegun always returned with game both before and after you've hunted in the same forest! I'm too old to hunt; and it will be your shame, not mine, when the word gets around and it is known for a fact that your father visits Olusegun's house simply because you cannot bring home meat from any hunt. And if you think I'm going to lose the habit of chewing meat simply because I was unfortunate enough to have you for a son, then you must be grossly mistaken."

The young men who might have been tempted to dislike Olusegun because of their parents' often unfair comparisons usually knew that Olusegun would be the first to discourage the practice if it were in his power. The men were always conscious of his good nature and comradely ways and they loved him. They realized that he could not help the fact that his natural superiority served as a constant reminder, especially to their parents, of their own inferiority. If they had anyone to blame, they knew it was not Olusegun, but the gods who had over-endowed him by comparison with them. But who were they, mere mortals, to blame the gods? How could they know that the gods did not have some special designs that were beneficial to the community and to themselves by so generously endowing him with talents? And who knew if he were not some god visiting the world in disguise? The ways of the gods, their elders had told them, had always been inscrutable. In any case, everyone agreed that Olusegun was a jolly good fellow and they loved him and respected him.

Naturally, every single girl in the village had secretly prayed that Olusegun would choose her for his wife. It was the custom of the people of the village to reserve final judgment concerning how wise a young person could be considered to be, until he or she had selected a marital partner. This was the ultimate yardstick and it was well founded. Many were the promising men and women who had been ruined by selecting the wrong partners. Equally surprising were the instances of those whose fortunes had vastly improved as a result of the wise selection of marital partners. In the case of Olusegun and Adunke, the unanimous verdict was that both had chosen most wisely.

As the darkness of the encroaching night rapidly enveloped the village, Adunke's father sat in his oil-lamp-lit hut, discussing certain farm matters with his oldest son while his three wives were preparing dinner in the kitchen, located in a shed behind the hut. Voices in conversation and the sounds of the pestle pounding yam in the mortar floated from the kitchen to the hut where father and son were conversing. Suddenly and for no reason that the son could discern, the father started frowning, got up abruptly, and walked rapidly toward the kitchen. The initial scattered pattern of pestle beating yam against the mortar had soon settled into a definite rhythm and the father had recognized this rhythm as belonging to Adunke. He had barely reached the kitchen when he started shouting his orders.

"Adunke, stop pounding at once and hand over that pestle to your sister. And you," he said, pointing to Adunke's mother, "follow me." Both obeyed his commands, and the food preparation was carried on by the two other wives, their daughters, and Adunke's sister. One woman dexterously and bare-handedly fished pieces of boiling hot yam, cocoyam, and cassava from the pot, periodically dipping the hand into a bowl of cold water. The other woman and the girls peeled the hot pieces with swift movements of bare hands and kitchen knives and deposited the peeled pieces into the mortar for Adunke's sister to pound. A different pounding rhythm was soon established.

"Tell me," Adunke's father demanded of his wife on reaching the hut, where he sat while the wife respectfully stood in front of him, "why it is now, when the *Omoge* is only four days away, that you must subject Adunke to the rigor of yam pounding? And just when all other mothers in the village are treating their girls, whom they had hidden in fattening rooms, like eggs? Is it that you have forgotten that Adunke's age group is performing the ceremonies this year?" His voice was angry.

"No, I have not forgotten," the wife calmly replied. "And it is precisely to enhance her beauty that I am subjecting her to some exercise."

"You mean other women are foolish and you're the only wise mother in the village?"

"Not so."

"Then explain yourself, woman." His voice was still angry.

"Right from childhood, and unlike many in her age group," the wife began to explain, "Adunke has been feeding well, perhaps too well. And now, she has a tiny little bit of fat to shed in order to be in her best shape for the festival."

The wife paused, and when she realized from the husband's silence that he had recognized her wisdom, she changed her serious tone and added in a jovial manner:

"You should credit me with more sense than you seem to do. After all, I am the expert in this matter. And I dare say I can still steal the show from your daughter if it comes to feminine beauty!" She accompanied her last statement with an exaggerated wriggling of her waist and a simulated coy smile.

"Foolish woman!" the husband said, starting to smile and chuckle. "How would I know you had no secret designs to make Adunke look haggard so some other girls could snatch Olusegun. And who knows, you might be thinking of capturing him yourself. After all, you've just said that old women never lose their dreams of beauty!" He laughed hilariously.

"So, I'm now an old woman, and all I had all this time was only a dream of beauty, not beauty itself?" she remarked in a feigned voice of annoyance. She then moved her body, which was indeed good-looking, with a more accentuated coquettishness.

"Foolish woman!" he said again, more amused. "If you quench that lamp with your movement, how do you expect me to see the beauty you're so anxious to exhibit?" He laughed happily, enjoying her teasing, as he dismissed her.

"Foolish woman!" he repeated endearingly. "Make sure my food isn't late and that Adunke gets rid of that extra fat or else you might find yourself looking for a new husband after the festival!"

She too was laughing and was further teasing him by consciously wriggling her shapely buttocks as she walked back to the kitchen.

Although he was yet in his early fifties, Adunke's father was already accorded the respect and recognition reserved for elders. His words, which were always carefully considered before being spoken, carried weight at the village gathering. Any visitor to the village could easily mistake him for the village chief, considering the special distinction villagers accorded him. Amazingly for a Yoruba community, however, this village operated a republican system of communal organization which had no room for chiefs and kings.

History had it that the village was founded by a rebellious age group who, resenting the tyranny of the ruler of their former community, had moved out to a new settlement. The village had remained faithful to its democratic spirit, and at the village commune everybody had the right to contribute to discussions. Even though the wisdom of the elders usually guided such discussions, decisions were always democratically arrived at and executed. But for the regard in which the villagers held their republican system of communal organization, Adunke's father could have claimed easily and without fear of contradiction the unused title of *oba*, village head. But he did not even nurse such an ambition. He was so much part of the traditions and beliefs of the village that the thought never occurred to him. As it was, he was a most happy man, enjoying the reputation of having the largest barn of yams, of being the owner of many treasures, husband of the most beautiful wives, and father of many children.

Three days to the festival, mothers decorated their daughters with traditional wood saps, drawing on the bodies intricate linear and curved patterns that assumed a lusciously dark blue coloration the next day when the sap had dyed firmly into the skin. After the body had been polished with fried palm kernel oil following a bath of cold water, the patterns glowed brilliantly to enhance the natural beauty of the skin. A day to the festival, mothers engaged expert hair dressers to plait befitting hair styles for their girls. Nails were neatly clipped, the usually whitish edges and the under of the feet were dyed glossy blue or shining red, and the body was massaged for the last time into a delicate suppleness to enhance the beauty of body movements especially during the dancing that would take place at the festival arena.

The usual anticipatory anxiety preceding an important event was felt across the village, but it was generally believed that the festival this time would surpass those of the previous years. This was considered inevitable since more than ever before the age group performing the ceremony boasted of more beauties and highly acclaimed girls, with Adunke raising the greatest expectations. The male age group that was to accompany and guard the celebrants during their day-long stay at the forest spring, located a good distance from the village, was no less distinguished since Olusegun was a member and the leader. The role of men as guards was a recent development, otherwise *Omoge* had been an exclusively female affair. The element was introduced less than a decade before the present festival when news reached the village that at some distant part of the land, a whole age group of unarmed and unguarded girls, engaged in a similar ceremony, had been forcefully taken away by armed men who traded in human beings.

Although expectations were high, none could deny that the festival of the year immediately preceding this one was a success. Then, as always, this age-old annual traditional beauty pageant, involving only girls of the age group whose turn it was to get married, had taken weeks of preparation. On the appointed day, the girls had departed the village at cockcrow for the forest spring around which the bush had been previously cleared to admit ample sunshine. Since men were introduced into the festival, they had gradually evolved a special role for themselves. At this time, their function consisted of labor and police duties. Hence on the third day to the festival, the select age group of boys who were only two to three years older than the girls, had gone to clear the ceremonial grounds around the spring. At a safe distance from, but within ear-shot of the spring, they had also prepared a piece of land where they would camp while the girls performed their rituals.

As was now the practice, the boys divided themselves into two parties on the morning of the festival. At the first cockcrow, the first party went ahead to ensure that the grounds of the spring were safe. The girls then followed and thereafter the second party of boys walked at a discreet distance behind. On arrival, the girls went to the ceremonial grounds at the spring and the boys joined the vanguard party at their own camp. By then the sun had risen.

During the morning and the afternoon while the girls carried out their ceremonies at the spring, the boys at intervals sent parties each consisting of five persons into the forest to hunt. Those remaining in the camp played, sang, danced, and generally kept themselves busy but ever alert to the security situation at the spring. When the first hunting party returned, another was sent into the forest. The hunters also understood their duty to include that of scouting the surrounding grounds to ensure security. The game killed during the hunts was roasted and shared into two and the greater half was sent to the girls during meals. On this sacred day, the men were strictly forbidden the taking of alcoholic drinks, quarrelling with one another, or having any sort of verbal or physical contacts with the girls, and serious penalties awaited whoever transgressed anyone of these rules.

As usual, the girls after performing their strictly religious rituals on arrival at the spring in the morning, had nothing to do but relax and play all day. They feasted, renewed old acquaintance, made new friends, and rehearsed their songs and dances. At each girl's choice, she swam and bathed in the stream flowing below the spring. The girls emerged from the water each time to continue pampering and decorating their bodies. A few hours to sunset, they put finishing touches to their body and hair adornments and started preparing to return to the village.

On seeing these signs of preparation, the boys sent a party consisting of a fifth of their number to the village, where they arrived, singing martial songs and doing the hunter's dance. They circled the square a few times and then dispersed. The village, which had been awaiting this signal of the imminent return of the girls, doubled its preparations of welcome.

Not long after this, the girls arrived at the outskirts and the awaiting festive village greeted them with much jubilation and joyous ovation. Commencing the much expected triumphal entry in this annual pageant parade, the girls in measured dignified dancing steps, slowly entered the village in a single file, leaving ample room between one another. Except for the decorative horsehair and other hairy animal tails which they held in their hands to accentuate the voluptuous rhythm of arm and body movements as they danced, each girl was absolutely nude. In another century, when Western civilization would have started making future generations ashamed of their culture, earrings, necklaces, and wide-looping sets of beads would be worn on the necks to cover as much of the provocatively firm and full breasts as was possible. More massive rolls of beads would be similarly packed on the waists and hips to hide, again as much as possible, the lower private regions of the luscious virgins. At this earlier time, however, the long single file of nude girls with seductively fresh skins elaborately decorated with dark intricate patterns made with wood saps, progressed in gorgeously slow movements, rhythmically responding to the melodious songs which they sang in accompaniment to the soft music supplied by seven boys. The second party of the boys who had guarded them had followed as soon as they had left the spring. Having seen them safely back to the village, they had dispersed, leaving only seven drummers to provide music during the pageant parade.

The village huts were symmetrically arranged in straight rows around a central square the size of an adult's farm, where village meetings and festivals were held. The square, dotted at regular intervals with shade trees, was also the place where old men regularly relaxed, leisurely smoking long tobacco pipes and sharing jokes, or seriously discussing private or public affairs. In the evenings and on work-free days, young men also met there to play the *ayo* game and exchange the latest news about farming, hunting, and their social life. Behind the front row of huts on either side of the square, there was another row separated by a broad walkway in which twenty men could stand shoulder-to-shoulder. The walkways had to be wide in order to accommodate the stream of festive crowds that often spilled over from the square in celebrative dances during festivities. Spaciousness was particularly prized during vigorous acrobatic performances by masquerades, some of whom often held long and slender tree branches with which they pursued young boys and girls who had to have sufficient room to be able to flee to safety. On the third side of the square, a single fifth row of huts stood, joining the rows on both the sunrise and sunset sides. The unjoined fourth side of the square narrowed into a major track which connected the village to surrounding villages, all of which would in the future grow to form the single town *Odenla*.

The long single file of celebrating beauties gradually snaked its ceremonial way from the edge of the village to the central square amidst more public cheers and jubilations. In as unostentatious a way as possible and in order to fake a naturalness of endowment, each girl consciously modulated her singing voice and calibrated the rhythm of her dancing body in order to maximally enhance her appeals. Those who did not have to simulate physical appeal because they were naturally attractive, danced as if they were merely basking with joyful abandon in the generosity of nature, whereas every single one of their movements was equally calculated to accentuate their natural beauty.

As they were cheered and praised, the girls knew that all eyes, especially those of the young men and their parents waiting to finalize the selection of marital partners, were on them. Men planning second, third or fourth marriages were also watching from the wings. Usually after this festival, old engagements were often broken or reconfirmed, new ones were made, and marriages were celebrated. Between the previous and the present festival, as many as eight girls were known to have lost their fiancees to other girls whose beauty, discovered during the ceremonial parade, had captivated the new lovers. A remarkably shy and self-effacing girl, who previously had received scant attention because her beauty had remained hidden from view until it was forced into the open by the festival, was said to be still finding ways of coping with the avalanche of suitors who started courting her after the ceremony. Of course, there had always been girls who, because they were fully conscious of their natural endowments, had regularly gone with great confidence to the festival, knowing that it could only enhance their reputation. This was the spirit in which Adunke went with the forty five others of her age group to the spring in the early hours on the day of the present festival.

Olusegun was the leader of the first party of men that preceded the celebrants to the spring in the early morning of the day of the pageant. The girls followed, and were followed in turn by the second party of men. Everything went as it should. The weather was excellent and everyone anticipated a fabulous day. While the girls were performing their ceremonies at the spring and the boys were keeping a watchful eye on them, the village was agog with preliminary celebrations. Visits were exchanged, there was eating and drinking, women were forever cooking, frying, or serving food, men drank palm wine and played the *ayo* game, and children ran and frolicked in the square—all in anticipation of the evening when the men and girls would return and the real celebration would commence.

The evening could not come early enough for some people, but those who knew how to wait said it was too early to expect the celebrants home.

"I believe it is considerably past the time for the arrival of the girls," observed an evidently impatient man.

"I think it is just getting to the time they should start preparing to arrive," countered an obviously patient villager.

The sun moved inexorably towards setting and everyone agreed that the boys and girls had over-delayed their return.

"But why are you all fretting?" asked a usually respected villager. "Don't you remember that the groups we're expecting this time are not like any groups we had expected in the recent past? Have you forgotten we're speaking of girls and boys led by the extraordinary pair of Adunke and Olusegun?"

"Yes, indeed. You must be right," readily agreed a listener. "Certainly with our courageous Olusegun at the head of the guards, no harm can possibly come to our girls."

"Now that you've said it," commented another villager, "I believe we've all been worrying for nothing. The girls and the boys, wanting to distinguish themselves as they deserve to be, must be preparing some surprise package to thrill us on their return."

"I think you're right," agreed some villagers.

"You must be right," agreed yet others.

Anxiety temporarily disappeared. There was renewed hope. Excitement returned and again villagers waited patiently.

But sunset rapidly descended and darkness commenced to envelop the horizon, and still there were no signs of the celebrants. Panic suddenly took hold of everyone. A party of hunters was swiftly despatched to investigate. They hurried, trying to take advantage of the last rays of the dwindling light, and still hoping to meet the celebrants on their way back. They did not meet anyone until they got to the spring, and those they met there or around were either dead or incapable of coherent speech. It was, however, not difficult to observe in the fading light that there had been a great battle on the grounds. Everywhere was trampled over, pieces of clothing and traditional items of girl's toiletry were scattered, and traces of blood were all over the place. A trail of violently trodden path, apparently taken by the attackers and the village boys, was soon discovered by the hunters and followed.

Darkness soon swiftly and completely enveloped the forest. The hunters could no longer see. Meanwhile, a second despatch of men from the village had arrived at the spring with lighted torches. The men also saw the signs of battle and the path earlier taken by the hunters. They followed the path after sending a couple of men to report back to the village. The men with torches and the hunters soon met and they both continued trailing the path of violence. Before long, they came across a badly wounded man from the village who narrated to them what had happened.

Just about the time the first party of men were to be sent to the village to signal the imminent return of the girls, a sudden chorus of alarm was raised at the spring. The village boys rushed to the scene to discover that the girls all to the last person had been rounded up by armed men who promptly started chaining them to long poles. The five hunters who had been scouting were also in chains, having been surprised, captured and gagged by the attackers. The men from the village charged but were stopped by iron sticks that released fiery stones which killed instantly. The village men tried to retreat in order to regroup and organize a strategy of attack, but they discovered to their horror that other men with the same iron sticks releasing instant death had cut off their retreat. Nonetheless, the men of the village still charged, fighting ferociously along with Olusegun, who killed a couple of the enemies, exhibiting the most courage. But all too soon, the fight was over and all the men from the village who had not been killed were chained together like the girls. The attackers marched their reluctant captives away in a single file. The wounded man, who narrated the story of what had happened, was one of those who had been cut loose from the chain of bondage and dropped on the way to die because they retarded the march and were too severely wounded to survive.

The villagers, who were badly shaken by the experience, finally recovered only to discover that the incident was just the beginning episode in a continued confrontation with a new phenomenon called the slave trade. Their lives were never again the same, having been drastically readjusted to a new harsh reality. Those like Adunke and Olusegun who survived the middle passage and ended up in the different plantations of America had to deal with an even more severe form of structural adjustment to their lives in a horribly brutal and alien environment, an adjustment that proved ineffective before the monumental and unending pain of the incompleteness they felt at having been torn away from the core of their essence. Day or night, and as they helped build a technologically better world, they dreamed of the delayed but inevitable reunion with the core from which they had been so violently hyphenated at the length of a seemingly endless ocean.

Parable of the
Great Grandson

(i)

When the first white man, a Roman Catholic priest, came to the town of *Odenla* in the year eighteen hundred and eighty five, Shangomola— farmer, high priest of *Shango,* and psychiatrist—was, of course, one of those who had gone to listen to him. It was not merely to satisfy the curiosity of seeing for the first time the white man about whom so many rumors had already circulated, but more importantly to hear what the apostle of the new religion had come to say. As *Shango's* high priest, Shangomola was both an interested party and an important personality whose opinion on the new religion would be sought by the community.

Located in the deep interior far from the coastal ports, *Odenla* was one of the last places in Western Nigeria to be reached by the white man. However, news of his imminent arrival had preceded him by about a whole decade. Traders and travellers were the first to report his slow but steady penetration of the interior. Converted Yoruba preachers from the coastal towns were the next to appear. They spoke of the coming of the white man no longer as a remote event but as an imminent reality, and as if to confirm the news, they

started preaching bold heresies against the sacred gods. Their sacri-
legious pronouncements against the gods went unpunished largely
because reports of what the colonial government had done to com-
munities which had manhandled such heretical messengers were well
known. The white man would not have his messengers trifled with
and did not mind using excessive force to prove the point. Moreover,
at this time only inconsequential individuals at the fringe of society
took these black heretics seriously.

Except for the negligible converts, life in *Odenla* went on as
usual. Shangomola like everybody else continued to cultivate his land
and tend his crops. Traditional religious observances went on unin-
terrupted. Worshippers of *Shango*, god of thunder and lightning,
brought their offerings as always to Shangomola's shrine. Nobody
touched a person, house, or object that had been struck by lightning
until Shangomola had performed the traditional ceremony of cleansing. And only the stupid rain-maker, courting the wrath of *Shango* and
a violent fiery death, would try to induce rain without first consult-
ing *Shango's* high priest in order to seek his cooperation and blessing. Nobody at the time had exhibited the symptoms of madness,
otherwise such a person as usual would have been referred to the high
priest's professional psychiatric care. In fact, the latest joke in town
was for Shangomola's peers to tease him by accusing him of professional negligence and complacency for not attempting to cure the
black preachers and their converts of their religious madness.

When these same black preachers suddenly one day announced
the long-expected arrival of their white master, the *Shango* high priest
was one of those who had gone to the square to verify if indeed the
white man's religion had been faithfully represented by the black
messengers. The latter had preached in a manner which suggested
that the only way to win converts was to disparage and antagonize
all other beliefs. Without hearing it from the horse's own mouth, it
was difficult to believe the foolish statements made by the black
preachers. These were statements that seemed to suggest that the
white man was yet to discover the wisdom of religious tolerance.
Shangomola knew that for centuries this wisdom had been the philosophical basis of the traditional religious belief system among his people. It had never occurred to him as the priest of *Shango* that the
followers of *Ogun*, for instance, should not enjoy freedom of worship.
He found it equally hard to believe that the white man did not know
that *Shango, Ogun, Osun, Esu,* and the other deities were the multi-

ple members of the single godhead *Eledunmare,* and that to insult any deity was to offend *Eledunmare* Himself. He was sure that the black preachers must have misrepresented the white man, who was reputed to be a clever man by those who had seen his handiwork. This was the state of mind of Shangomola and of the vast majority of the people from the community who had gone to listen to the white priest who spoke through an interpreter.

Shangomola in the end came away from the meeting in utter disbelief. His worst fears about the white man and his new religion were not only confirmed, but new revelations also showed that the situation was even worse than he had at first imagined. In the old ways, when a man died, his widows both old and young were shared as nominal or real wives among his male relations to ensure that no widow or her children remained uncared for and without a breadwinner. To Shangomola's dismay, the white man's religion insisted that a man must marry only one wife and that anyone who had married many should repudiate all but one of his wives. Apparently, it did not matter if the abandoned wives suffered neglect while the husband, for whom they had preserved their virginity until marriage, to whom they had remained eternally faithful in marriage, and with whom they had planned their entire life and future after marriage, was still alive! Shangomola was appalled and could not understand why any religion should preach such wickedness. And such ignorance too, he believed. The gods his people had worshipped faithfully for centuries were pronounced as fake by the white man who urged on the people the abomination of burning the material symbols of the gods, and the abominators were then supposed to turn to the only authentic religion—that of the white man! All this was beyond belief for Shangomola who at the appropriate time, like so many others, spoke against what he termed the religion of blindness and wickedness. His verdict was that the white man's religion was not even good enough to be added to the old religion, let alone substituted as replacement.

Not surprisingly, the majority of the people continued to follow their old ways and the new religion won only few converts even after it had established a permanent mission in the town with a resident white priest supported by black preachers and an array of staff and servants. The reputation of the new religion was further damaged when other denominations came and established their own missions in the town. A war of rivalry started between the different factions as each claimed exclusiveness to authenticity and salvation. As time went on, each mission built a school to promote its own brand of righteousness, and the schools were usually situated on the same grounds that contained the mission house and the church building. This proved a good strategy on the part of the missions, even if the expected result was not instantaneous. While the philosophy and theology of the new religion did not appeal to the vast majority of the people of *Odenla* for contradicting what they perceived as the essence of true religion, the lure of the mission schools proved in the end irresistible. The colonial administration which had been only a remote echo in *Odenla*, became a constant presence soon after the churches arrived. Immediately it was realized that the colonial administration had come to stay, and that no one could prosper in the new political dispensation without first acquiring knowledge through the white man's system of education, the mission schools started gradually to witness increased enrollment. At this stage, even the Sango high priest Shangomola, who was already an old man, saw the wisdom in sending his youngest child, Dada, to school. Since attendance at a mission school was contingent on the acceptance of the mission's own brand of Christian righteousness, Dada soon learned his catechism, passed the test on the fundamental tenets of Catholicism, and got baptized. Even though the old high priest stubbornly continued to call him Dada, he was now everywhere in official documents known as Peter.

(ii)

Shangomola had selected Dada, aged thirteen, because he was the brightest among his youngest children and he was sure to assimilate well whatever the white man's school had to teach. He developed quick understanding as a child. Quite early, he played and did things intelligently. As a small boy, he performed well the little tasks he was usually assigned whenever he accompanied his parents to the farm. As he grew older, he developed a keen interest in farming and it soon became evident that he had what they called the green thumb. The crops that he planted always grew and he carefully tended them into mature plants. The parents had in fact begun to look forward with pride to the future because they knew he was sure to develop into a successful farmer and a respected, well-integrated member of the community, with wives and several children. However, when it became obvious to Shangomola that he had to send one of his children to school, Dada who for his intelligence was the obvious choice, was reluctantly selected.

Dada, now known in school and church and by his peers as Peter, proved expectedly a quick learner. He combined intelligence with good manners and achieved a level of amiability that attracted good notice by the school, church, and colonial authorities and which made him liked by fellow students. From year to year, he moved easily from one level to another until he reached the highest attainable in an educational system whose sole purpose at this stage was to produce clerks, school teachers, catechists, stewards, cooks, and other workers who would facilitate the effective colonial and church penetration and administration of the territory.

As soon as he graduated, Peter, who was now twenty, was posted as steward to the Catholic parish mission. The parish priest had always wanted a brilliant young man who could effectively run the administration of the mission house and generally serve the mission in other capacities. Since his duties required residency, Peter moved from his house from where he had attended school as a day student to the boys' quarters, situated a good three hundred yards away from the mission house where the Reverend Father, the priest, lived.

Every morning, Peter got up quite early from his room in the boys' quarters, woke up the cook in the adjoining room and proceeded with him to the mission house. While the cook prepared boiled water for the Rev. Father's bath, Peter selected and neatly laid out clean underwear, socks, handkerchiefs, a pair of shorts, a shirt, and a cassock. He polished the shoes and made sure that everything the Reverend Father needed for the morning mass was ready. If the altar boys were late or absent, he also assisted at mass; otherwise, he merely attended as any other faithful Christian. He left the church immediately after service to go to the mission house to lay the Reverend Father's breakfast. He waited on the Father at table and did whatever the Father commanded. After breakfast, he gathered used towels, cassocks, and other clothes worn the previous day and handed them over to the washerman. The latter first meticulously disinfected the clothes, almost all of which were made of white cotton material, by boiling them in a big metal drum before washing, starching, drying, and ironing them to immaculate whiteness. Peter also supervised the gardener who maintained the flower beds and the grounds of the mission house which was situated on a picturesque, airy, rock plateau, overlooking a green belt of forested valley.

Before setting out every weekday morning for school inspection, preaching in the outdistricts, house visits to the faithful, or any other missionary activities, the Father first instructed Peter on what to do in his absence. Often it was an errand either to the house of the resident colonial administrator or to the traditional ruler's palace. Other times, the instruction concerned some arrangement that had to be made with the local laity in respect of some religious or social functions. Or it could be to arrange baptism, confirmation, marriage or burial ceremony. Often it was to help the catechists organize instructional classes or choir practice. It was Peter also who regularly obtained and supplied to the mission cook the vegetables, tubers, meat, fruits and other local constituents of the priest's meals which were freely, happily, and generously given by parishioners. The priest himself arranged with the provincial headquarters of his mission for the regular supply of the European items in his meals like biscuits, flour, tinned fish, corn beef, tea, coffee, canned milk, sugar, soft and alcoholic drinks, and sweets.

Peter often accompanied the priest on his distant outdistrict outings which could last a day or a week as the need demanded. Because Peter understood the vernacular idiom of the region better than the interpreters who came from the coastal towns, he was regularly used as interpreter during these outings. Peter who was always the first person to wake in the morning was also the last to retire to bed at night in the mission establishment. Apart from waiting on the Father at dinner as he did at breakfast and lunch, he had to stay to put everything neatly away after the Rev. Father had retired. Not infrequently, the priest would receive local visitors in the evenings and Peter was also usually called upon to act as interpreter on those occasions.

Peter satisfactorily carried out his duties from year to year and the priests, who regularly replaced one another at the periodic intervals determined by their superior, the diocesan bishop, increased his salary and paid glowing tributes to his sense of duty, efficiency, good Christian behavior and pleasant disposition. He grew in years; his polygamous father, Shangomola, the high priest of *Shango*, died and was buried; he married in the church and had Christian children; the children attended the mission school and showed great intelligence and promise of reaching the highest level of educational attainment which, luckily, had steadily expanded since Peter himself went to school.

Peter worked with devotion, serving the church, and looked forward to old age and retirement. Suddenly, his immediate older brother by the same mother fell sick and died, leaving children and three wives. The ages of the latter ranged in the middle and late twenties.

According to long-standing tradition, the responsibilities of the deceased brother were shared among his surviving brothers. The task of taking care of the needs of one of the wives and her three children fell to Peter, who was compelled to accept this new burden despite the objections he raised on the ground of the rules of his Christian religion. Deep down, Peter recognized the justice in the dismissal by the elders of his religious arguments as constituting illegitimate excuse for abandoning traditional moral obligations. If he ignored his own deceased brother's responsibilities, who did he expect to shoulder them? Having thus convinced himself of the morality of tradition in this matter, Peter succumbed.

Subsequently, Peter arranged for his brother's children, allocated to his care, to start attending school just like his own children. He carried on his duties in the mission as faithfully and efficiently as before, but he now visited home a little more frequently. The community was proud of him and frequently pointed him out to others as a role model who knew how to combine respect for tradition with faithfulness to the new belief. Thinking that Peter had the sanction of his church for his harmonious marriage of religious cultures and the new family arrangements, some in the community had in fact started saying that the new religion might, after all, not be as inconsiderate and intolerant as it had initially presented itself. However, this favorable impression would not continue for long because one afternoon in the third month of carrying out his additional family duties, Peter was rudely confronted by the Reverend Father himself.

"Boy, come over here at once!" the priest had angrily commanded. Peter was at the time in the company of a catechist and a group of boys and girls with whom he was conducting choir practice under the shade of a mango tree. Although older people like the cook and the gardener were regularly called "boy" by the priest, neither Peter nor the catechist had previously been so addressed in deference to their education. Although, on the other hand, they never enjoyed the respect of being called by their own names, they were given the distinction of being addressed by their professions. Thus, the call hailing them was either "Catechist!" or "Steward!" Consequently, it was not certain this time who the priest wanted. The confusion did not last for too long, however, because the priest himself soon clarified the matter.

"I say, Steward, you come here at once!"

Peter walked quickly over, wondering what he had done to deserve the insult which the priest had intentionally made very obvious. Having only too frequently seen such disrespect regularly shown to his kind by the priests and their white visitors on the slightest provocation, he would not have been surprised if he was being subjected to this indignity simply because of some minor forgetfulness or error on his part.

"You hypocrite!" the priest had challenged him as soon as Peter got to where the priest was standing. "Do you think you can for long continue to deceive God? You pretend here to be a model Christian, whereas you had since secretly reverted to your old, filthy, heathenish barbarism. You were not being clever, boy, but only consciously compounding your mortal sins each time you had returned to defile this holy ground with the corruption from the secret visit to the foul bed of your concubine ...."

"Please, Father, let me explain," Peter interrupted, but the Reverend Father would not listen to him.

"I will not listen to your lies," the Father said. "You people are adept at lying. The least you can do is to stop desecrating this House of God with your adulterous presence. So go at once and pack and do not let me catch a glimpse of you or of any member of your family anywhere near here at nightfall. Be gone." Having said this, the priest, who throughout the interview had stood at a discreet distance as if Peter had a contagious disease, walked briskly away in righteous indignation.

(iii)

Peter, who was now thirty-five, did not have long to regret the abrupt end to his fifteen years of service to the Catholic mission before he was employed as court clerk by the colonial administration. Because of a dire need for educated Africans, the colonial officer ignored the negative recommendations of the priest, Peter's last employer, on the ground that Peter's offence was religious not criminal. Since Peter had not registered his marriage to his dead brother's wife, he was technically not guilty of bigamy. In any case, the colonial administration had more to worry about than the enforcement of the law of bigamy in Africa at this time. Moreover, there was the incontrovertible fact that, despite condemning Peter for what he called Peter's "hypocritical adulterousness," the priest had admitted that Peter was an intelligent and efficient worker. Peter's own four children and the three by his brother who had all been banned from further attendance at the Catholic mission school on the ground that they would be bad examples to others, were registered on the colonial officer's recommendation at the Anglican mission school.

The community hero-worshipped Peter because he refused to heed the advice of fellow Christians who suggested he show remorse for his sins by repudiating his brother's widow in order that he might be readmitted to the holy Catholic fold. Although Peter did not reject his Christian beliefs, he certainly became more sympathetic to traditional cultural and religious practices than his Catholic education had permitted him in the past. Peter was now nominally an Anglican, but in reality he no longer believed in the superiority of any one kind of organized religion, Christian or traditional. What was really important, he believed, was to sincerely try living an honest, humane life as good people had always done in the land before the appearance of the white man. If there was really a heaven, then one would certainly be admitted after death. And if there were none, one would have had the happiness emanating from the consciousness that one was living right.

Peter worked for another twenty years as a successful court clerk before retiring from the colonial administration at the age of fifty five. His children from his two wives, who altogether numbered eleven, had various levels of education. Some became school teachers, some clerical and administrative officers in the colonial service, and some went into politics or business. His oldest son, John Shangomola, who was aged forty at the time of Nigeria's independence in 1960, was one of the Nigerians who had been carefully groomed for the post of Permanent Secretary in the Federal Civil Service by the departing colonial administration.

John Sangomola's second son, born in 1950 and named after his grandfather as Peter Dada Shangomola, turned out to be a very brilliant student. With very little help from his influential father, he won a Commonwealth scholarship to study medicine in Britain. He completed his studies with distinction and in record time and was vigorously courted with postgraduate fellowships by several British medical schools. He settled in the end for a medical college based in London where he had since become a distinguished surgeon, married with two children to a pretty English lady with a Ph.D in English from Oxford.

Dr. Peter Dada Shangomola was seriously contemplating returning to Nigeria in 1989 for no other reason than to cure a persistently recurring attack of home sickness, but he was advised against it by his father. Hadn't he heard, his father wanted to know, that something called a Structural Adjustment Program (SAP) was "brain-draining" Nigerian doctors and scholars to Saudi Arabia, Europe, and America? No, he was to take it easy for the time being, because SAP time was the wrong time for any young man who was not already a millionaire to attempt returning from overseas to Nigeria. If his home sickness was that acute, his father advised, let him come on a visit with his family. In fact, SAP time, the father informed him, was the ideal time to visit because his wallet-full of British pounds will transform into a bag-full of Nigerian nairas on arrival.

The good son took his father's good advice and visited in January 1990 to escape the Northern cold and enjoy an early taste of the sun. He spent two weeks in Lagos and then moved with his family, wife and two children, to their home town *Odenla* where they had planned to stay for another fortnight in order to give his family a taste of his origin and Africa's authentic hinterland. However, the very next day after their arrival in *Odenla*, they hurriedly packed and returned to Lagos. Today, long after their visit, the most amusing joke circulating in *Odenla* is of the spectacular sudden appearance of the white wife and mulatto children of the great grandson of the high priest Shangomola. Much is made of the fact that the great, great grandchildren could only communicate with the local people by smiles and through interpreters very much in the manner of the first white man, a Catholic priest, whose appearance in *Odenla* in the year eighteen hundred and eighty five is still a living history. The anecdote usually arouses an explosion of uncontrollable laughter among *Odenla's* inhabitants whenever it is further disclosed that neither the wife nor the two children of the great grandson of the Shango high priest could correctly pronounce even their own family name—Shangomola!

Mother and Son

"No Sweetness Here" — (Ama Atta Aidoo)

(i)

The closer the end of the school year, the broader the smile the mother perceived on the face of life. Life rarely smiled at her. In fact, she had known only hardships all her days.

It all began when her loving parents forced her into an early marriage with a man she didn't love. To make matters worse, her husband wielded sufficient local influence to thwart her two successive attempts to divorce him. There was nothing else she could do. Some people in her situation attempted suicide, but life was too precious for her to try that. She resigned herself and started bearing him children. Just like his four other wives.

Thirty five years had passed. And now for the first time life was a bosom friend, all smiles, patting her lovingly on the shoulder and warming her heart with the good news. In three months her eldest son would be completing his studies in a university in some strange, distant land and would be returning home.

Six years he had been away. And six years she had waited anxiously, praying day and night to her ancestors, the household gods, and the Almighty above to watch over him. And now he was due to come home to her! How good life is! One only needs to know how to be patient when it is hard.

The mother certainly knew how to be patient. And her patience was tried a great deal. When both her parents died in their mid-forties, she was left alone in the world. No brothers, no sisters. Her husband was just her husband. Nothing more. If he had loved her, if he had made her his favorite wife, perhaps she might have overcome her initial objections. But she gave birth to a daughter with her heart still revolting against him. She was actually contemplating a third attempt at divorce when her first son arrived. She was resigned completely.

In a polygamous family where your husband, even when he wished, did not possess the means to provide for you and your children, a son was the greatest blessing you could expect. He was your future protection, your breadwinner, and the consolation of your old age.

But a son was not only a blessing. At least not now anymore. When she was young, it was all so simple. You were born to a farmer to be a farmer. The more children there were, the more hands to help on the farm. You could marry as many wives as you wished, and have as many children as survived childhood. Today it is all different. You have to educate your children, education being now the only sure way to economic and social survival. And she was determined to survive. So she sent her son to school.

She spared nothing. But it soon reached the stage when she could no longer change the children's clothes at Christmas, much less her own. She went into debt, but all the same, failure was imminent. The husband could bear it no longer, so he called his oldest sons, and said to them:

"Look, this woman has tried enough. Her son too is bright. We must help them. After all, if they make it, they'll remember us."

But all their help amounted to little, and the boy would still have dropped out of secondary school, had not the local Catholic Teachers' Association offered a helping hand.

The mother smiled for the first time in many years that day when her son completed his secondary education. Eight months later, when she was thinking her son was only eighty miles away at his teaching post, she suddenly received a telegram from the capital. It was her son informing her that he was leaving that day on a government scholarship for some strange, distant land.

The news spread like wild fire. The local people rejoiced with her, were proud of her, and showered her with compliments. She fidgeted in embarrassment at all the well deserved praises. Life was suddenly smiling on her. Really broadly. They said scholarships were not easy to get, and the foreign ones less so.

Her only worry was for his protection in that unknown and unheard-of land. She also feared the evil eye on her other children, and on herself. After all, it was not for nothing that the old people say *"Ko seni to feni foro afi ori eni."*

And now it has all come too true. Some malicious person has secretly left an evil medicine in some place for her unsuspecting foot. A dull persistent pain began to torment her in her right foot. She ran up and down for a cure. It would not go away. He had a letter written to her son about it. As she had known beforehand, her skeptical son denied it had anything to do with medicine. He suggested a natural cause, advised a practical step, and sent some means. The pain persisted.

Three years have passed since he left home and his former classmates who attended the National University have recently obtained their first degrees. They have all settled down and it was already a month since they started providing for themselves and their next of kin. That, of course, was the purpose of education: to yield financial return. What good was it otherwise?

The mother became restless for her son. If he were home, he would know a way to cure her foot. The permanent pain was sapping her energy. She tired very easily, and she could no longer work as much as she used to do. Suddenly it dawned on her that she was already older than when her parents died. A certain kind of fear gripped her. If only her son would come home soon.

To make matters worse, people began to ask embarrassing questions as to when her son was expected back. She hated to answer such questions. Who could tell? People might begin to say that she was boasting that her son was doing something more serious than their own sons. If only her son would come home soon.

But he did not. It did not depend on him. So he had written. That was the order of things in that strange land. One had to spend six years. It was not for nothing that the thought of him going so far away had worried her in the beginning.

But she would wait three more years. She had waited three already. Waiting for a better life had always been her lot. She was patient. She would be patient some more. What were three years to the fifty and more years she had waited already?

And now, didn't she say that six years would finally come around! Just look, only three months are left. Everything says there are only three more months to wait:

The burning midday sun pleads gently with her: "Tolerate me a little bit more, mother," it says. "Your son will soon be protecting you from the million sharp arrows of my merciless heat."

The moon, smiling broadly, teases her good-naturedly: "Sharpen your imagination, mother, for soon you'll have all the time to stay out late and dream under my caressing light. There will no longer be any need to hurry early to your hard mud bed for fear of waking late in the morning for work."

Young twigs bend mischievously across her paths to the plots and plead with childish simplicity: "Let's caress your legs, mother, a little more lingeringly, for your son will soon be claiming you from us."

Everything was kind and sweet to her. Even her foot didn't hurt her as much. The days swiftly went by. She hid her tumultuously radiant inner life from outsiders while she secretly and intricately planned a welcome for her son. In the middle of the last month, she left the farm for town. Some twenty miles away.

At the end of the month, instead of her son, a letter arrived. Perhaps he was regretting he had to delay a week. No, not a week, not a month, not even a year, but three years! Would they kindly reread the letter to her? No, there was no mistake. Another three years! No, it couldn't be. The family council agreed that it couldn't be. He was to be immediately written and told to come home at once.

The mother was still walking about, dazed, when two days later another letter arrived. Especially for her. Unlike the aerogramme letter to the whole family, this one was in an envelope. Pages and pages. They had been written a whole week earlier, yet the aerogramme had arrived faster. How could she have failed to realize that the other letter was not meant for her? How could she have allowed herself to be persuaded even for a moment that her son would ever behave selfishly? Some had even gone so far as to suggest that it was some woman holding him prisoner. How little they knew of her son!

She had the letter reread to her. This was him for sure. Her son. Full of love and consideration. Detailed explanations of everything, with the pros and cons clearly stated. He was going to write the family in a week or so, but that would be merely a formality. His decision would depend solely on what she thought. He knew exactly what he was asking, and would she honestly let him know whether or not she could stand another three years?

Of course, she could. Let them write and tell him she definitely could. After all, what did she want for herself? She even felt ashamed of her former impatience. Wasn't her real concern for her children and grandchildren, and were not his plans in the best interest of these? Surely, she could wait.

Again the local people were inquisitive to the point of embarrassment. Then suddenly, as if by general agreement, they stopped mentioning her son's name in their conversations any time she joined their company. She knew they were being delicate in their concern for her. But what right had they to treat her son that way? As if he were some queer disease, as if he were some person to be ashamed of. And what was most disturbing, they were treating him with that silent scorn reserved for only those who die young.

Dying young, God forbid, was of course awfully shameful. What right had anyone to die young? Giving birth to you was a responsibility your parents fulfilled both to their own parents and to you. In turn you were duty bound to live to old age, and to give birth to others. That was how life was meant to be. Dying young was shirking one's responsibilities, it was cheating. Cheats were to be scorned. To even mention their names in conversation was to do them honor. But her son was not a cheat.

The mother did not at all like what was happening. Yet she dared not protest. She wanted to assert that her son had done nothing wrong, but how dare she bring up her own son in a conversation of this type when she had not been asked? Who would stand such a breach of propriety? When she could no longer bear it, she left town and went to the farm. Twenty miles away.

A year passed. Two more to wait. The mother was again on the farm. This time as a necessity, rather than to hide a tumultuous joy or conceal a crushing shame. She was weeding. She looked up at the sky to see if it was time to eat lunch. It was yet early. The sun was only just approaching the center of the sky. She bent down and resumed her work.

Her stomach kept arguing with her, but one must not trust it. The sun was more reliable. After a while, she raised herself up again to check the position of the sun. Suddenly, everything went blank. She staggered, struggling to maintain her balance. She made it to a tree and leaned on its trunk. The dizziness following her fainting spell lasted a little while more, and then was replaced by fear.

She was not afraid for herself. She wanted nothing, and was in absolute peace with her self. She could die now happily, knowing her children and grandchildren would be provided for when her son returned. Her fear was for him. In his last letter, he had pleaded: "Mother, please take care of yourself. You know there is nothing that would give me more happiness than to be able to show my appreciation for all you suffered on my account...."

Even in this she wished not to fail him. But the uncertainty of it all made her feel helpless. She gripped the trunk of the tree she was leaning on in desperation, wishing painfully she could dictate her own terms to nature. But the hard bark of the tree scratched her brutally, as if purposely pushing her away. The mother recoiled in anger. As she did so, she cast a suspicious glance upwards to make sure a treacherous dry branch was not at that moment threatening to crash down on her. The branches of that tree, and those of other trees around, were motionless. Nature seemed to look on in absolute unconcern. As if she was not there. She poignantly wished she could hug her son just then.

(ii)

"Ah, no! The thought I cannot bear,
And if God please my life to spare
I hope I shall reward thy care,
My mother." — (Ann Taylor).

After reading the letter he had received, the son lost desire for everything. Extremely disturbed, he climbed into his bed in order to give rein to his thoughts. In case he fell asleep, he took the precaution to set the alarm clock.

Two hours later the son jumped into a half-lying-down, half-sitting-up position at the sudden ringing of the alarm. Throwing his weight on his right elbow, he leaned sideways, his left hand mechanically reaching for the clock on a chest of drawers. At the same time, he tried to wake up.

But a frightening awareness suddenly crashed into his consciousness. He was neither asleep nor awake. Worse still, he felt he existed in two separate parts, with no knowledge of where his real self was located.

Nothing at all was real, except for a vague, vast spaciousness where he seemed to be timelessly hanging. He felt an unbearable incompleteness. He wanted desperately to be complete. He struggled for his own unity, fearing and wondering where he was, what was happening, if he was dreaming, if he would ever wake up again. An eternity of incompleteness, of uncertainty, of fear....

Suddenly he felt that he was there again, united, complete. His weight was resting on his right elbow, his left index finger was still pressing down the knob of the alarm clock. It was hardly sixteen seconds since hearing the first alarm signals. He was in a half-lying-down, half-sitting-up position, with the sheets covering half his body. He jumped quickly out of bed, afraid of a repetition of the frightening experience. Half awake, he sank into an armchair. He was perspiring, and his heart was beating rapidly.

He tried to understand what had just happened, but comprehended nothing. Still afraid, he muttered: "Oh God, I hope nothing happens to me."

That precisely was the thing. Nothing must happen to him. How could it? When he did not belong to himself? When he was only his own keeper?

Many times before now he had wished he were his own master, that he could live and die as it pleased him. But that was wishful thinking. He knew too that for the foreseeable future he would have to watch carefully over his charge, taking no risks, exposing him to no danger. He would have to avoid all adventures in a country where only the adventurous foreigner could be happy. All adventures involved some risks; every school child knew that, but he dared not take any risks.

He was strict over his charge too. No going out alone late at night. No visiting noisy pubs where fights could break out. Always swallow insults to avoid a brawl. These and many more. And, of course, the heart too must be tamed. Whoever heard that a keeper married off his charge against the expressed wishes of the owners?

Only the other day he had met a girl. What a girl! All day long his heart had pumped and thumped. It seemed to him that his happiness was smiling on him. All he had to do to find out was to take the phone and arrange a date. If he was not rejected outright, then an involved relationship might develop. The latter was even worse than the former, being doomed from the very beginning. The experience was always most painful. No, he remained a good keeper and did not take even that risk.

And that was exactly what anybody in his position would do. The opposite could be possible only if he were not his mother's son, only if the memory of twenty eight years of mutual selfless love between mother and son could be erased clean off his consciousness.

And that was impossible. Nothing could ever remove the impressions of the December afternoon twenty two years ago, when he suddenly woke up from the slumber of a careless childhood and grew up all in a day.

Then he was sitting in the shade under a tree, taking care of his nine-month-old sister. His mother was weeding a yam plot, the merciless midday sun piercing her back with millions of hazy arrows.

She had been singing for quite a while. At first her voice easily scaled the undulations of the road. Then the undulations gave way to little hillocks, which were in turn replaced by massive hills that were followed by insurmountable, slippery, rocky mountains. The son trailed along, observing the painful climb. Then it reached a point when it seemed his six-year-old heart would burst, seeing the agony of the effort. He cried out in a compassionate, mournful entreaty:

"Please, mother, do not cry anymore."

And he himself started crying.

Until then it had not occurred to the mother that she was crying. She rubbed her cheeks and was surprised to find her bare arms wet with tears. She immediately abandoned her hoe, wiped her face clean of tears, and hurried to her crying son, when it was she herself who needed consoling.

"You see, I'm not crying. Who tells you I'm crying? I was only singing," she said, caressing his head and pressing him close to her high thigh.

No more words passed between them, but similar thoughts revolved in their minds.

He had failed the end-of-year school examination that December. His father had concluded he was a dullard and decided not to waste any money on him. Until then the boy had not known what school meant. He had taken it for a place to play and be merry. And, indeed, he was sent there when he was only approaching his fifth year, partly because he was a fast growing child, but more because he was an unbearably stubborn, mischievous imp at home. Since the average age of his class was seven, some instinct told the child that school was only a way of getting rid of him. So he got his zero on every sum and failed all examinations, and was not the least bothered. But now his father had proved that his instinct was all wrong. The mother didn't think so. She believed that they the parents, and not the child, were to blame for prematurely sending him to school. Now that the child has actually reached the proper age to start attending school, he ought to be given his proper chance.

The mother and father had quarrelled over something shortly after that. Perhaps it was also because of this that the father had detained his older sister at home when their mother needed her help on the farm.

The son knew that his mother was his only hope of returning to school.

"Mother, please say you'll send me back to school," he pleaded later when they had left the farm plot and were on their way to their farm hut. He looked up at her with an expression of pain.

"I will, I will, my son, my own heart. Only promise me you'll never fail again."

Both sides kept their promises. A miracle happened in the case of the boy. Not only did he never fail afterwards, he was always one of the best two in class. The mother lived only for her promise. She went half-naked; she went half-starved; she sacrificed her health fulfilling this promise.

All along the son watched the mother climb the undulations, the hillocks, the massive hills, and the insurmountable, slippery, rocky mountains on the path of her promise. And all unknown to himself his heart grew larger and larger until a bottomless well of love for her, his brothers and sisters was sunk forever deep in his heart. He burned with the steady fire of this boundless love, and lived with a single purpose before him: to make it in life, comfort his mother's old age, and do for his brothers and sisters what their mother had done for him.

This was a heavy responsibility, the details of which had the effect of stripping him clean of his individual freedom, of making him, a twenty-eight-year-old man, not his own master, but only his own keeper. And as a good keeper, he was always in constant fear and anxiety lest he should fail in his duties both to his charge and to the owners.

He could, of course, deny his charge, liberate himself, and be the sole master of his life. But then, would he be able to erase the memory of a dedicated mother? Would he be able to....

What's the use of enumerating the impossible? Besides, he was only too well aware that life had meaning for him only because these responsibilities existed. His goals, his constant striving constituted his happiness. Thus, however difficult it was, however much he complained, he was vaguely aware of some basic happiness.

Now it was all different. He had known what it meant to be in dire need of money, what it meant to be hungry, to be lonely. But all these were nothing compared to the feelings that now dominated him.

He reached for the letter from under the alarm clock and once more read his youngest brother's girlish handwriting.

"Mother is sick. The worst may happen any moment. You had better come home, although she said...."

Each word struck terror into his heart. As if he was hearing the deliberate voice of the judge pronounce:

"You are a murderer. Your guilt has been proved beyond reasonable doubts. You are condemned to...."

"But I had not meant to," he defended. He did not believe himself.

"She said she could wait," he tried to reassure himself.

"But you should have known better," someone countered. That was the truth but he still waved his last argument, hoping for a miracle.

"I knew all right, but I was counting on her psychological preparedness to do the trick. Besides, it was in the best interest of all the family that I got my higher degree."

"The psychology worked all right, and it is surely in her best interest now," someone mocked.

As if to counter this mocking, he grabbed the letter again and began to read.

"Mother is sick...."

"She is only sick," he emphasized as if trying to convince someone.

It didn't work.

He remembered fifteen years earlier when he was in his last year in the Primary School and a letter of this type had been dictated to him. Then the son, an apprentice to a watch repairer, was only about two hundred miles away.

Villagers are wise. Why cause an unnecessary pain, anyway,

when the worst has already happened? A little hope left in the doom might do the trick. Mother is only sick.

The room could no longer contain him. He started walking up and down the sidewalk on his street. The neighbors saw him once, twice, thrice.... An unusual exercise. They grew suspicious. One fellow came out to check if the doors of his car were properly locked. Night fell. Neighbors' dogs barked at regular intervals all through the night. When they were driving to work in the morning, the neighbors saw him dressed exactly as yesterday and walking in the same way. He said not a word. He did not answer greetings either. When the dogs began to bark the second night, the neighbor with the car called the police.

Part Two

The Heresies

The Apprentice

Obatunde survived the ordeal of his apprenticeship thanks to his having a past. A past that traced back to Oba. Oba, his great grandfather. Oba, the illustrious. The wise ruler.

Obatunde had the choice of going to school, but he would not. He had witnessed the fate of his grandfather and this had decided his position once and for all.

He was a mere child at the time. His grandfather was at the height of his glorious rule. Life was moving on meaningfully just as it had during the reign of the illustrious Oba, his father. He enjoyed the love and respect of his subjects. Peace and quiet dominated. Contentedness and accord prevailed....

Then suddenly they came. Uninvited. As if that was not enough, they said his grandfather did not know how to rule. His grandfather! The offspring of the illustrious Oba! One whose ability to rule in times of poverty and riches, sedition and peace, pestilence and health had become a legend!

And that was not all. Life, they claimed, was being led not altogether the way it should. Everything had to be overhauled. A new beginning was necessary....

And indeed they immediately commenced to effect the changes. With inhuman speed and haste. Obatunde, a mere child, saw it all.

He was confused by it, but he had no difficulty in understanding the cause of the premature death of his grandfather. He was horrified to realize that his father could not become king after his grandfather. No one would continue the rule of Oba, his illustrious great grandfather! He himself could have no pretensions....

In spite of this, they wanted him to go to school! To put his stamp on those changes and proclaim them God-sent and just! Him, Obatunde, the great grandchild of Oba, the wise ruler! *Never. Never. Never.* His royal blood revolted vehemently against the suggestion to succumb to an inglorious domination, to the worship of a false god. And he was a mere child.

But he had to do something. He had been born. What did it matter that the times were like this? Was that not the purpose of his birth? To make meaning of a life like this?

Obatunde took up the challenge. He decided to become a master blacksmith and his years of apprenticeship soon began. Life was going to be meaningful from now on. So he thought.

He was mistaken, for it was only then that his troubles actually began. He was hardly a year old with Omotaiye, his master, when the latter called him aside:

"Obatunde," he began in his gentle, humane voice, "you know I love you like a son, and that I have the highest respect for you as an apprentice. I believe you will make my name great yet, and that is why I'm grieved at what I see in your works lately."

Obatunde loved and respected his master, so it was with deep concern he heard these words. Emotions choked his voice as he said:

"May I know what grieves you, master? If it is within my power, I will do everything to alleviate it."

"When I look at the hoes, cutlasses, knives and other implements you forge," the master continued, "they show no definite character; they are amorphous. However minutely I scrutinize them, they fail to reflect the lessons I have been at pains to teach you. I have repeatedly said that your aim should be to forge a hoe that is both practical and cheap. What's the use of a beautiful hoe if everybody, *e v e r y b o d y,* cannot afford it? As things are going now, people will soon begin to say that you are the apprentice of Omotola."

For Omotaiye to say that the work of his apprentice resembled that from Omotola's workshop was the most serious criticism that Omotaiye could ever make against anyone that studied under him. Obatunde knew this and was troubled. He agreed essentially with his master, but he felt within himself the existence of something. Something exclusively his own which he could bring to the forging of a hoe that would make that hoe more practical, more cheap, more attainable and more beautiful. For this reason he experimented endlessly. Little by little he approached his goal. But the closer he got to this goal, the more the hoes he forged differed from those of his master. He had noticed this and was worried, but he had hoped that his master would not perceive the difference. But alas....

"Master," Obatunde began excusing himself, "you know I'm not imitating Omotola. I'm only trying to forge hoes my own way."

"You're talking nonsense, my boy. That's an old story. And it's all they say when they are actually turning against you. But for you to do that! You, whom I love so! You, who are...." The master was overpowered with emotions and could not continue. In a moment, however, he straightened up and added in a stern, uncompromising voice: "Remember, if you choose to be my enemy, don't forget: an enemy is an enemy."

Obatunde was frightened, but he managed to say:

"I'm not your enemy, master."

He was not believed. Life subsequently became difficult for him in his master's workshop. He tried to kill his initiative, but all the same, anything he forged bore a quality that was not his master's. Something unmistakably his own. In the eyes of his master, however, this something showed increasing resemblance to the quality distinguishing products from Omotola's workshop. The master's love for his apprentice changed into dislike, and soon it matured into enmity. Explanations didn't help. They only made things worse.

During this trying period Obatunde sought to survive the cruel reality of his apprenticeship by escaping into his past. He recollected the stories of his illustrious family as they were narrated to him by his mother. It was as if he had witnessed the events with his own eyes. Every night he dreamt of Oba, his great grandfather, the wise ruler. He thrilled with joy in his sleep as he relived the last heroic deed of Oba.

"The plague came suddenly," his mother had told him. "Oba was ruling at the time. There was plenty. People were contented. Life was simple and meaningful. Then suddenly the plague.

"The effects were swift and disastrous. People died in hundreds. Soon it became evident that the population would be wiped out. It was then the wise men consulted the oracles.

'the Spirit of the land had been offended. an unusual atonement

demanded. *a man must sacrifice himself in expiation. no influence exerted. the choice completely voluntary. sole motivation—the individual's love for the people. otherwise the Spirit would not be appeased.'* Thus spoke all the oracles.

"For a long time nobody volunteered. People began dying in thousands. It was then, early one morning, that Oba, the wise ruler, the beloved of his subjects, called his family together. He hugged everyone with tender emotions and then announced his intentions.

"Words spread like a wild fire. Dissuasions increased every second. The population consulted together and sent a delegation. 'Is it not enough that we should die like chickens? Must we also be left without a ruler? And a ruler like you? We would all die rather than lose you.' These and many more were the words spoken. But Oba would not be dissuaded.

"It was a gloomy afternoon. Sorrow was on every heart; fear written on every face. Oba, the illustrious, the wise ruler, walked calmly towards the Hill. Absolute silence reigned in the crowd of aggrieved subjects escorting their beloved ruler on his last journey. The gloomy silence was frequently pierced by heart-rending wailings that gushed forth from the desolate houses on the route. The bereaved mourned their dead. Almost at every step someone from the procession, who only a moment ago had been most actively alive, would suddenly stiffen and drop stone dead. Like a rotten dry wood blown down by the wind. Sorrow on every heart. Fear on every face.

"Oba hastened his steps. Soon he was at the edge of the precipice. Unspeakable fear gripped everyone as the wise ruler jumped the Hill. He vanished without a trace into the bottomless abyss.

"The Spirit of the land was pacified. A new life began. Your grandfather assumed the throne. He followed the foot steps of Oba, his illustrious father, your great grandfather, the pride of the land. Once again the land knew splendor, subjects enjoyed plenty and comfort, life was simple and meaningful....

"Then suddenly they came. Uninvited.... You know the rest of the story, my son." Thus concluded his mother. Her voice sad. Very sad.

His mother had died seven years before, but the recollection of this story made him feel as if she was once again alive; as if he himself was once more a six-year-old carefree child. He was happy, relieved by the knowledge that life had once been meaningful, that once there had been a king who knew how to rule, that one day there might yet be another....

These thoughts were Obatunde's succor in the trying days of his apprenticeship. Omotaiye soon came to hate him bitterly, and before long the master asked his apprentice to leave. Without a certificate, testifying to the completion of his apprenticeship, Obatunde could not practice. This even though he felt he had acquired enough of the basics on which he could build to be a great master himself. Thus he found himself on the other side of the river, knocking on Omotola's door.

"Eh, see who is here! Come in. Come right in. Haven't I always said you're welcome in my house? Yes.... Really!... I'm not actually surprised, though. Isn't it common knowledge that Omotaiye is mad? I'm happy it happened, though. I have always dreamt of having an apprentice like you. With me, it will be completely different. You'll be free to forge any kinds of hoes, cutlasses, knives, and other implements exactly the way you like. Absolutely free. Of course, who would think of forging a hoe that is not durable as well as being beautiful? People know they are buying quality and, naturally, they're prepared to pay something extra. Why worry about *e v e r y   T o m ,   D i c k , a n d   H a r r y* ? Where is the guarantee that even if their Dick could afford our hoe, he'll make good use of it? So, you see, you're welcome. Come right in."

This was how Obatunde was received by Omotola, the archenemy of Omotaiye, his former master. Obatunde understood the condition of his acceptance, but he also knew that he had been promised freedom. However, a year had hardly gone by when Omotola called him for an explanation.

"I have given you sufficient time to get rid of the nonsense with which Omotaiye has stuffed your head. Apparently, you're in no hurry. Perhaps you don't even intend to.... Yes, yes, I quite understand. Far more than you suppose. You all say that even at the very moment you're going against one. But it's an old game, my boy, and the answer is as old as the Bible. You cannot serve two masters. So, you're either for me or against me. And it's time you declared your stand."

Again life became bitter for Obatunde. What was he to do? He had sought to safeguard his honor by refusing to go to school, but had ended up making things more difficult. And all because in this cruel time it was enough to be caught in the family quarrels of strangers to be denied one's dignity, one's rights.

Omotaiye and Omotola, as rumor had it, were twins. Identical twins. This was apparent to even the most casual observer. One was as tall and athletic as the other, as healthy and boisterous as the other, as courageous and ambitious as the other, as talented and hard-working as the other, as tempered and diplomatic as the other, as good a master as the other, as....

One could go on forever enumerating the points of similarity. Yet these twins would be the very first to deny the existence of any such similarities, of any kind of relationship. They had never known each other from Adam. Didn't you study Geography? How could you possibly confuse someone who lives on this side of the river with the one on the other side? Can't you recognize the signs of the time? Then, why won't you differentiate between the road that leads forward into the future from the one that goes backward into the past?...

The arguments were inexhaustible.

Obatunde heard it all and was at a loss to explain that it was his least desire to serve as an arbiter in a family quarrel, that he did not want to be caught in the crossfire between two brothers, that his sole desire was to be a smith, a simple smith, forging hoes his own way and dreaming of Oba, the wise ruler, his great grandfather, when the going was tough.

Was that asking too much? Obatunde could not tell. He knew only that this was a trying time and he wished he would survive it.

The Gods Will Call Again

It was already half past seven and Iwalewa would be coming any moment, so I hurried out of the house without even tasting the pepper soup I had made. However, since I must have my pepper soup, I stopped by a *buka* on the way to my office.

"How are you today?" the service girl greeted.

"I'm fine, thanks," I said automatically, but then immediately I started wondering why she should have said that. This was my first visit to the buka and I had never met her before. I looked at her to make sure I was right and there I had my second surprise. She was smiling. That kind of a smile with a question mark which you see on the face of someone who expects to be recognized. I could not recognize her, so I dismissed her. Like you dismiss the smiles of airline stewardesses, secretaries, salesgirls, the caressing voices of telephone operators, the appeals of magazine cover girls, the charms of sexy television commercial women....

Halfway through my pepper soup, my eyes wandered aimlessly about the room and suddenly rested on her standing behind the counter. She was watching me and smiling. Familiarly. As if she had lost me for these so many years and there I was at last! So confident that I have finally come to stay. Her face was radiant with joy.

Watching her, I too began to feel relaxed. Completely at ease. As if I had been waiting for her all my life and there at last she was....

When I realized what was happening, I panicked, quickly swallowed the rest of my soup, and hurried out.

She smiled goodbye. With that confident assurance of an understanding wife. No matter how you storm out of the house, you will return to her. You love her more than you love anyone else.

I was frightened and I hastened my steps. It was such a great relief to start thinking about Iwalewa.

She would be in my apartment by now. Iwalewa! People have never ceased congratulating me for finding a girl like her. Iwalewa! The goddess of the town. One whose beauty and good manners had captured all the men. Bachelors and married men alike. Iwalewa!

"What are you doing to the poor girl?" Bode once had asked with pain in his voice. "Why don't you tell her you don't want her? Maybe she will finally begin to pay attention to those who really need her." Love was torturing him.

"Who said I don't need her? Haven't I told you we are getting married?"

"Getting married! Without love!"

That really got me mad. I was already damned tired of people preaching love as the only healthy basis for marriage. Like they knew what love was!

"Do you think we can go on like this?" Iwalewa too, had asked just last week.

"Like what?"

"Don't you feel you don't love me enough?"

"Must we go over this again?" I said, irritated.

For more than three months Iwalewa had used all the tricks in book, trying to get me to propose. Finally, a couple of weeks ago I got to seriously think about it. I wasn't in love with her. That was for sure. But I had my theory about marriage. Love hasn't got to start it. Love can come later. You live together. You get used to each other. Attachment develops. And before you know it.... Provided, of course, the characters are compatible. Iwalewa and I were compatible, all right. Besides, she adored me and she was sure to make a good wife. So I proposed to her.

And would you believe it? Iwalewa, who had been goading me to death about making the proposal, turned round and wanted to know if I loved her well enough!

I told her the whole truth, but it turned out that she knew it all along. Yet a week had not passed by when again she wanted to know if we could go through marriage like this.

I don't like people to be unreasonable. Hence I got mad at her and said irritably:

"Must we go over this again?"

"I guess I should be grateful I found the man I love, anyway. One cannot expect the ideal to happen all the time!"

That was how she settled the matter. This was reasonable to me, too. As a matter of fact, I thought of her already as my wife. I didn't see anything wrong if I didn't want to see her as often as she wanted to see me. She didn't see anything wrong with it either. In all probability she would patiently stay in my apartment this evening till I come back. That was what she had always done and I had come to expect it.

So what right had a *buka* girl to behave as if we had known each other for ages? So confident that I would come back to her even though I was seeing her for the first time and I didn't even know her name!

At twelve midnight I had closed my office door and driven home. Sure enough, Iwalewa was waiting.

"How was your appointment with professor Mawanu?"

"Marvelous!"

She laughed.

"I love you just the same," she said, hugging and kissing me.

Now, you see that! And some buka girl thought she could insinuate some far-fetched pretensions! Wonders would never cease.

The greatest wonder, however, was yet to come when, less than a week later, instead of making my own pepper soup, I found myself going to that *buka*. Curiosity, you know. And pride, too. To show her she had not intimidated me. After all, I was a man. And this was Africa.

As I walked in, the *buka* girl smiled. The smile with a mildly reproaching question mark. The kind you see on the face of your understanding wife, wordlessly reproving you: *Now, dear, didn't I say there was no need to walk out on me? But it's nice of you to have come back so soon. And don't feel bad about it. I understand. Nerves. Nerves. Nobody is above nerves. Kiss me gently, now, honey. Or say something sweet. Or simply look at me tenderly....*

I looked at her tenderly. Pacified, she smiled broadly. I was happy. She served my pepper soup. I took it to the table. Relaxed. Perfectly at peace. Capable of doing anything. Anything. Become the president. Command the whole world, the seas, the moons, the suns.... Anything. Oh, what harmony! What joy! What happiness!

Suddenly I was jerked awake as out of a trance. Terrified, I literally flew out of the *buka*. All the same, I managed to catch her expressive smile:

You're coming around, all right. Even sooner than I had expected. And you'll be back. Make no mistake about that.

"Nonsense!" I said to that as I shook myself thoroughly awake out of the spell.

Nonetheless, I went there the following day. And the day after. Her name was Ife. Ife Amorari.

One evening I took her out. That same evening I told Iwalewa everything. She was very nice about it. And the next thing I heard was that Iwalewa had got married! Not to Bode, as everybody had expected, but to some old mathematics professor. People said Iwalewa did it out of spite, but people say a lot of things, and what can they see but the externals? I felt bad, but Iwalewa had told me not to be worried about her. Anyway, there was no time to brood much over it, for I was soon very busy arranging for my own marriage.

I had never thought I would be marrying that soon. A year or two I had in mind. But it got so I could not live by myself any longer. I felt I ought to have Ife around me all the time. When I told her this, she said we were going to get married sooner or later anyway and she saw no reason why it couldn't be right then. I was so much in need of her that the full implications of what she said escaped me.

When we broke the news to her parents, her father was overjoyed. Not so her mother. It was like telling old news. She knew it all along. Which reminds me of the day Ife introduced me to them.

Her father greeted me warmly, enthusiastically, trying to make a good impression so his daughter wouldn't lose a prospective husband. Eagerness and uncertainty were written all over him. With her mother it was all different.

"Don't mind my husband. After all, what do men know?" she had said mysteriously.

It was apparent she had wanted to say more, but felt it was useless. *What can men understand, anyway?* her behavior implied. I could see in her eyes that she had known since the day I was born that I would be her son-in-law. *So why get excited over that which has been settled since time immemorial? And I have always liked you any-way,* her manner seemed to proclaim.

"Feel at home, Segun," she said aloud, pronouncing my name with fluency and familiarity, as if she had been using it since the day I was named.

I panicked. But Ife was sweet. Besides, her father's uncertainty offered comforting company.

So, it was not a surprise to me that her mother took the news of our decision to get married as a thing she had known all along.

Ife wanted a wedding according to native laws and customs. That appealed to the innermost depths of my being also. I remembered the beauty of those ceremonies. A wedding used to last for days and everybody, adults and children alike, participated. A joyous drama which was repeated again when one died at a respectable old age. Second only to the annual ancestor worship, initiation ceremonies, harvest festivities. Such grace, such poetry, such power that used to adorn and elevate men!....

"I prefer a court and church wedding," I said brutally.

"Why?" Ife asked.

Her mouth was wide open as she looked sheepishly at me, expecting my explanation. I had never seen a person as shocked as she was all my life.

"I had a Western education and I want a Western wedding. It's as simple as that."

Ife surveyed me most carefully, and then shook her head up and down, up and down, slowly, slowly... When pity began to form in her eyes, I changed the topic. I wanted to see only love in those beautiful eyes.

So, we had our wedding in the church. When the priest asked us to confirm our vows with a kiss, we turned to each other, we embraced each other, and became glued to each other, in one unanimous testimony to the law of weightlessness, the elimination of time and space, the denial of existence, even in the form of thought....

The wedding was a great success. Everybody showered praises and good wishes on us because we had been very generous and had executed a wedding that befitted out class....

Late, late at night, after strangers had departed, followed respectively by acquaintances, friends, relatives and parents, and we were in bed, I turned to Ife with a demand:

"Now you've got to tell me the secret."

"Which secret?" she asked, smiling.

The same smile by which she made me understand the very first time I met her in the *buka* that we had met before, that I was sure to come back, that our marriage was already a foregone conclusion....

"The secret you share with your mother and from which you have excluded your father and me."

She smiled. The same smile that her mother had worn when she had as much as said: *What can men understand, anyway?*

"Why have I got to tell you, assuming I even know what you are talking about?" Ife demanded.

"Because in the church today you promised to share everything with me. I am your husband. And you know what I'm talking about."

"You are my husband all right, but what secret can I, a woman, possibly have that you, a man, does not possess? Men know everything. They even know about our so-called superior power of intuition, and they allow themselves to wonder at our incredible ability to be practical in the affairs of everyday life. So, my husband, what more do you want to know?"

She smiled.

"The secret," I insisted.

"If you're not afraid," she answered "to peep at the reality behind the cliches, then follow me and I'll reveal to you that to which you've been blind."

"Whoever says a man is afraid!" I said with courage. Ife looked at me with love in her eyes and held my hands....

... the cave was warm and safe until the night the snake sneaked in and bit us. we ached, we pained, we swelled up and died. the gods had called several times before, but never as suddenly as on this occasion. our spirits roamed the forests and hovered over the caves for more than a century because we had no kin. then we found deserving strangers and lived again, and met again...

...this time we lived to a ripe old age when the gods called. this time we had children, grandchildren, relatives, so our spirits didn't agonize in a century-long search. she found the granddaughter of her sister deserving, and I preferred to be the son of our first grandson..

...and we met again, cultivated the land, reared children, but no grandchildren, for I was only thirty when Ogun called. when Ogun calls, the man must follow. she was grieved. a widow so young. she lived twenty more years because of the children. then Orisha called. she was glad. but in any case when Orisha calls, the woman has to follow.

she chose to be the daughter of our first daughter. my spirit favored the wife of my youngest cousin, and so I was their first son...

...it took us a long time to meet this time. but we met again. finally. after years of schooling, after years of college, after years of roaming in foreign lands, where I lost my memory. and because I lost my memory, when I returned, I mistook her for another. but I found her again. eventually. Ogun shall call again. Orisha will call. they had called several times before. we must be prepared. else our spirits may know again the agony of a century-long, torturing search for deserving strangers...

...so this first night of our reunion, let me cooperate with you, my wife...

"If you're not afraid," she answered, "to peep at the reality behind the cliches, then follow me and I'll reveal to you that to which you've been blind."

"Whoever says a man is afraid!" I said with courage.

Ife looked at me with love in her eyes and held my hands....

The Hyde Park Preacher

(i)

As Ogunmola roamed the streets of London in search of a summer employment, he wondered if his ancestors were not laughing at him each time the slick and polite personnel managers asked him, smiling: "Sir, what can I do for you?" or each time, on stating his purpose, he heard their inevitable reply: "Sorry, sir, the job has just been taken. Call back tomorrow to see if anything has turned up." Ogunmola remained undaunted in spite of these replies. He had faced the music before and he knew all about it. He continued from one personnel office to another with the same results, but could not cease wondering what his ancestors thought about all this.

In fact, the previous day after another fruitless search for a job, he had gone to bed at night only to find himself in a dream, crawling into a cave where he confronted a prehistoric ancestor. The latter had asked him why he was seeking to locate ancestral caves. When he replied that he was seeking knowledge, the ancestor had laughed hilariously at him, scornfully asking: "To what modern good has your generation put the ancestral wisdom already at your disposal?" He had woke up from the dream even as the ancestor had continued to laugh in scorn.

The cave dream was not his first encounter with his ancestors. Each time he had been too preoccupied with the thoughts about how his ancestors judged his intentions and actions, he had invariably confronted them in his dreams. Now he did not know whether or not he should stop bothering himself, thinking about the way his ancestors judged the fact that he, Ogunmola, was offering himself as cheap labor in London and was everywhere being rejected. Deep down in him Ogunmola realized that he wanted to maintain a constant contact with his buried past; consequently, he did not actively discourage his mind lazily dwelling on the question as to how his ancestors judged his present mode of existence. He wondered if he could decide the question by what his father, who was still alive, thought? He knew his father would disapprove. His father had always disapproved. "It is wrong. It is wrong," the father had said vehemently each time they had discussed the matter. "You were meant to be the priest of *Ogun*. You were chosen. Your birth was special. Your name was special. How could you forget? How could you refuse?" His father had always remained sad and incommunicable after every such outburst. And he had good reason.

It happened many seasons ago. Then Ogunde, Ogunmola's father, was only a young man in his sixth moon of marriage. Ogunde's father had come to him one evening and informed him that the family elders had decided he should carry the ancestral mask in the coming harvest festivities. Ogunde had objected, pleading ignorance, unpreparedness, but even as he voiced his objections, he knew he wanted the honor and that, in any case, since the elders had decided, there was little he could do about it. To refuse under such circumstances was to prove that he was still an immature child in spite of his marriage.

Ogunde had been afraid of failure, yet he had been fascinated at the same time by the opportunity to officiate as the intermediary between his family and the village community on the one hand, and the ancestors on the other.

"But I don't know anything!" Ogunde had complained to his father.

"Don't worry, you will be taught," his father had reassured him.

After this conversation, Ogunde had started preparing himself spiritually for the coming communion with the ancestors, who were the intermediaries between man and the gods. The closer the date set for the harvest festival approached, the greater Ogunde's anxiety had increased. It had been all the more a burden because he had had to keep everything secret from his wife with whom he normally shared his intimate thoughts.

The day had arrived sunny, brilliant, encouraging, yet it had been with fear that Ogunde had gone very early in the morning to the sacred shrine, where the village elders had already been waiting. When all the young men had gathered, the elders, led by the high priest, began the rituals of the initiation into the secrets of ancestral representation. Step by step the initiation process, which the young man had imagined to consist simply in the donning of masks, had revealed itself to be an elaborate, all-day-long process of practical training in chanting songs and in perfecting their dance and acrobatic knowledge. Above all, it had been a most serious, soul-searching process of meditating and cleansing through incantations. Finally, it had involved a gradual transformation from the earthly to the ethereal, from the physical to the spiritual, until one felt the touch of communion with one's ancestor and was completely possessed by his spirit. Then and only then alone was one worthy to don the headgear of the ancestral mask and wear the bright yellow robe, made entirely out of flowing shreds of young palm fronds. It was then that one drank one's last portion of potent palm wine, tapped and brewed by a special process, that was a secret, known only to the high priest, who initiated young men into this sacred and holy ceremony, which was at once both a thanksgiving to the gods for a good harvest and a recognition of our indebtedness to the ancestors for having successfully mediated between man and the gods during the past year. It was only then that one performed the final act within the sacred shrine before emerging into the village. This involved the sacrificial severance with one single stroke of the cutlass the head of a dog, with whose blood one then anointed oneself in recognition of *Ogun*, the powerful and fateful god, who had made the communion between man and his ancestor possible by bridging the eternal gulf between the worlds of the living and the dead, and who will further facilitate the dialogue on behalf of man between the ancestors, the gods, and the Almighty.

Ogunde had been amazed at the transformation which had occurred within him: the ease with which his body had beautifully responded to the intricate rhythm of the drums, the way the chants and songs had flowed easily out of his mouth, the mysterious spiritual power he had felt to be at his command, the knowledge that he could heal or destroy, bless or curse, the realization that he was no longer himself but something more—all these were so new and so intoxicating that the young man had proceeded with confidence, along with the other masks, to the public arena to meet the villagers, who had been waiting for them all day. Now the sun was already going down in the sky.

The public aspect of the ceremony commenced. The audience, which consisted of inhabitants of that village as well as visitors from neighboring villages, flanked the rectangular public square. At one end, under a baobab tree, men naked to the waist and profusely sweating, beat vigorous and intricate rhythms on their drums. To the right of the drummers, under another tree, the masks sat on stones, waiting for the right moment. When it came, they all sprang up and yelled in a chorus as they ran to the drummers, in front of whom they lined out, and then jumped up three times in unison and with grace. Then they surged forward, spreading all over the arena and danced vigorously, rhythmically, and exquisitely. After a while they returned and sat again on the stones. Soon again the masks challenged one another in pairs to competitive acrobatic dances of somersaulting and fascinating leg movements. Drums and gongs and other percussion instruments sounded, blended, and echoed, creating a thrilling, overpowering music; drummers sweated and sang; the masks danced again and again; the audience watched and soon, overpowered by the pervading joyous mood, started clapping hands, singing, and dancing. The entire village—masks and men, visitors and citizens, young and old, women and men—became one harmonious festive rhythm that vigorously and invitingly echoed in adjoining villages. The aged and the sick moved out of inner rooms to front porches to partake in the communion. From outside more and more visitors poured into the village to share in the celebration.

When at last this public function of the festival ended, the masks disappeared to their respective family homes, in order to bring blessings to their relatives and to receive the requests of these relatives for the coming year. The young man proceeded to his home with new elation. At the door, he yelled three times in the deep guttural voice of ancestors to announce his arrival, and then started entering the house the only way spirits did: backwards. Once he had entered, he turned and walked forward like humans to the center of the compound, a yard separating the main building and the kitchen block, both of which joined in an unbroken rectangle. There once more he yelled joyously thrice and, dancing, started a song which proclaimed:

> Long have I wished to cross the river
> Separating our worlds
> To reassure you
> I have heard your prayers
> To inform you
> The gods listen to me
> The Almighty blesses you
> To tell you
> To do no evil
> To love and help the brothers and sisters
> For it is only thus
> Your labors will bear fruits
> Your roads will be safe
> And enemies will be impotent before you
> And you shall know more seasons
> And multiply in numbers
>
> I have come, I have come
> Rejoice with me
> Tell me this reunion is good
> Tell me all is well with you
> Let me know
> If any of the gods has offended you
> And I shall ask for retribution
> Before the gods and the Almighty
> Let me know what ails you
> And I shall seek immediate relief
> As I take your requests with me
> Across the river to the land of the spirits.

As soon as he stopped singing, each woman in the house took turn coming forward with her children and knelt before him. With offerings of *kola* floating in a melon fruit bowl of water and green *atete* leafs emersed in an earthen plate of *epo* stretched out before her, each woman announced her joys, her woes, and her requests. When it was the turn of his young wife, she came forward alone, having just been married and still childless. She wanted the gods to bless her with a male child, promising that if her request was granted, the child would be set aside for the priesthood of *Ogun*, to whose service he would dedicate his life. The ancestor rejoiced, yelling understanding and dancing around her in three circles. Then he bent low to anoint her as he had anointed all the other women. He smeared her forehead in *epo* with the aid of the *atete* and sprinkled her with water from the bowl with the *kola*. This completed, he danced once more around her three times, blessing her. It was then the head of the household, his father, brought the offerings of a hefty goat, a robust keg of palm wine, three big tubers of yam, and three kola nuts—all of which indicated that the year had been good. In years of poor harvest and misfortunes, lean or no offerings at all were made because if the gods and the ancestors could not take care of the living by assuring good harvest and preventing ill luck, then they too must starve and experience discomfort. The mask, ancestors' representative, accepted the offerings, chanted prayers over them, slaughtered the goat, sprinkled its blood all over the yard to purify the house, tilted the keg of palm wine and spilled some on the soil, broke a kola, and sliced off a piece from the yam tuber. After chanting final blessings, the ancestor departed, promising he would return when the seasons have turned full cycle. He exited the same way as he had entered: backwards. He performed the same rituals in the remaining four houses of the family before returning to the shrine in the grove behind the village. It was late in the evening and already dark.

When the young man returned home, his father smiled approval and he knew he had done well. The wife dodged his eyes and pretended not have missed him all day. Later, however, she cuddled closely to him in bed and embraced him more warmly and more passionately than she had ever done before. The young man guessed she too approved of him and was expressing this through her emotions, since it was taboo for her to know what had transpired that day of the return of the ancestors. That night his child was conceived and nine moons later was delivered. The child was named Ogunmola, so that when he grew up, he would always remember that he was the appointed, the one set aside for the ministry of *Ogun*, the god of transition, creativity and artistry, god of iron and war, guardian of the road, explorer, hunter, and custodian of the sacred oath.

When Ogunmola grew up, he resisted the path his parents had

chosen for him, in spite of their vehement protestations. He chose to go to school, rejecting the art of the blacksmith and the ministry of Ogun priesthood. And now he was roaming the streets of London, a strange city, in search of job to support himself in the process of acquiring a different vocation. No doubt, Ogunmola thought, his ancestors must be amused at the comic plight of this prodigal son, who had preferred the anonymity of a jobless, homeless itinerant to the dignity of *Ogun* priesthood. This doubt had assailed Ogunmola for several years and had plagued him with renewed vigor each time he faced difficulties in his chosen path. To make matters worse, his parents would not cease reminding him that it was never too late to return to the right path. It was perhaps to please his parents and satisfy some indefinable urge within him, that he had elected to study anthropology and to specialize in the definition of caves, as a means of retrieving the cultural history of his people. But of course, in spite of his explanations, his parents had considered this a poor compensation for the real thing—the high office of *Ogun* priesthood.

Ogunmola, however, remained intransigent. He was at peace with himself because he was somehow convinced that he had broken no trust, that no harm would come to him or his relatives, even though the latter were constantly and fatally expecting retributions from *Ogun*. Above all, without any explanations he could give, he was convinced that his ancestors were pleased with him, that he was fulfilling the purpose for which he had been born. Sometimes, however, he wavered in this confidence; any time this happened, he confronted accusations in his encounters with his ancestors, as occurred in his recent cave dream. But in the end, he always regained his confidence, and even now, as he roamed the streets of London in a fruitless search for a job, he knew that all was well.

(ii)

In the afternoon of the third day of combing London in search for a job, Ogunmola was hired as an assistant salesman by a cloth retailer who owned one of the rows of small stores lining the streets of Liverpool Market, East London. He was to report for work the following day. Relieved, Ogunmola celebrated his good fortune by ordering his first meal of the day, a plate of fish and chips. Still half-hungry, Ogunmola left the cafeteria, struggling to blunt his memory, which was stubbornly recalling the plentiful and tasteful meals of fresh organic vegetables, grains and tubers, daily served in his home in the village.

Ogunmola walked unhurriedly towards Central London. He observed as if seeing for the first time the faceless throngs, hurrying along the streets of London; the enormous glass windows, displaying disparate objects for sale; the endless streams of traffic that flowed in columns like soldiers and came suddenly to a stop as at a command; the red double-decker buses, covered with gaudy, bigger-than-life advertisements, speeding past as some unidentifiable monsters in a nightmare; the littleness of man, dwarfed into an insignificance less than that of a grain of salt beneath the imposing buildings, palaces, and monuments in that capital of the world, which worshipped things, things, things....

Tired, Ogunmola climbed onto the top of Temple underground train station and flumped into one of the park benches overloooking the river embankments. Below him a flower garden, spreading eastwards, presented a picture of ordered beauty. Small alleys wound around symmetrical beds of flowering celosias and geraniums, hibiscus and lantanas, marigolds and petunias, roses and salvias, tulips and zinnias. Small marble figures from Greek mythology, bathed in fountain waters, hid in cool corners of green grottoes. People lay drowsing on the grass, or strolled unhurriedly through the alleys. River Thames glistened under the sun, heaving gently as boats ploughed up and down its course. Ogunmola wondered if the waters of River Thames and the Niger ever met in the Great Ocean. He was curious as to what would happen if they did. Would the Thames contaminate the Niger with its industrial wastes, or would the latter purify the former of its pollutions?

Ogunmola wondered what the people in the village were doing that afternoon. He wanted to know what his life would have been like had he understood his calling in terms of his parents' beliefs. Were his own beliefs actually different from theirs? he pondered. His parents had maintained that life was complex enough for an *Ogun* high priest, one of those who had the burden of preserving the philosophy of the land, a philosophy they claimed was as authentic as that of any other land. Why did he think that it was necessary to make life even more complex? Was River Thames any better for industrial pollutions? Or was it because the poisoning bespoke of technological advancements? Could he be certain that the instrument of Western ethnographical and archeological historians would penetrate the secrets of his ancestral cave? If River Thames could handle its industrial poisoning, was there any assurance that the Niger would not spit its forth in fatal fumes across its banks to the destruction of the inhabitants? Could it be that he had failed to locate his ancestral cave while still at home simply because he had believed without questioning, that his native instruments were ill-equipped, not advanced enough for the task? Ogunmola shuddered as he conceived of the possibility, that he might actually have been systematically blindfolding himself while he had thought he was looking for the light. How would he confess this to his parents? Surely, they would laugh at him for having gone all the way to Sokoto to look for what was all the time in the pocket of his sokoto....

Ogunmola's reverie was interrupted by a rustling noise behind him. He reluctantly turned around. A shabby middle-aged tramp, wearing a winter overcoat in spite of the summer heat, was rummaging in the garbage cans in search of edibles, cigarette butts, and anything that could be useful. His hair, thickly caked in grease and dirt, spread disorderly like confused, mud-soaked ropes over his head. His thorn-like beard, studded with earth and pieces of trash, was powdered in grey dust. His white skin had gone multicolored under a yellow background. His small red eyes darted nervously from one object to another. As he came closer, a rancid stench from drink, sweat, and dirt preceded him. Ogunmola got up promptly from his bench, descended the stairs rapidly, and proceeded towards Trafalgar Square via Charring Cross. He rested a while at Trafalgar, watching tourists feed pigeons or pose with statutes and fountains for photographs. Ogunmola then strolled over to Piccadilly Circus to listen to music at a record shop. Later as Ogunmola walked through Oxford, he recollected his first impressions of that busiest street in London.

That was a Saturday evening five years before, during Ogunmola's first summer visit to Britain. What had struck him as most outstanding were not the beautiful squares and fountains, nor the attractive shop windows, nor the impressive architecture of old buildings, but the people who had populated that street. It was the first time Ogunmola had seen humans in their greatest number and variety within a given duration of time. His imagination was captured mainly by the diversities in the manners of dressing of those strolling in the street. Only a few middle-aged and elderly people wore conventional clothes. The overwhelming majority were teenagers and these were desperately seeking innovations in clothing. However, what exactly these innovations should be, they seemed to have no notion whatever. Consequently, there was total confusion. It was this confusion that had fascinated Ogunmola. There were all sorts of styles, most of which by Ogunmola's standards were simply crazy. Some wore rags and others wore practically nothing. What amazed Ogunmola the most was that those who were naked were actually in the majority. Yet in the midst of this confused hell, as Ogunmola had perceived life in Oxford Street, he identified what he regarded as heaven. Yes, heaven in hell! In the midst of that God-forsaken, crazy, confused street, two men bore witness to God, trying to rescue universal Christianity from its perverted Capitalist forms.

Now, Ogunmola smiled ironically to himself, remembering these impressions and how naively he had comprehended them. Oxford Street was no less crazy nor less confused now than it had been five years before when he first saw it, but this craziness and confusion no longer overwhelmed Ogunmola. He now perceived this chaos as a living evidence of the state of Western civilization, which was still pathetically doing its best to convince the world of its superiority. The sight of men, dressed in sacks and incessantly addressing passers-by, calling them to God, and carrying religious placards no longer aroused religious emotions in Ogunmola for he had already discovered the greatest paradox of the century. He wondered what his father would say, if he were to tell him that those who had declared themselves to be atheists were, as a matter of fact, more god-like than those who professed themselves to be Christians, followers of Christ, believers in God. Ogunmola walked through Oxford Street, trying to decipher what the omens portended. But he had not the pretensions nor the pomposity of the high priests of Western gods to divinate for an alien culture, even though he had those advantages derived from intimate knowledge, which the Western high priests never possessed while pontificating over other cultures. In any case, Ogunmola was no longer certain that he was still a priest. Could a blindfolded person be expected to lead anybody? Ogunmola got tired of Oxford Street. He wanted to be away from omens, whose meanings he could not interpret. He wanted open space, green leaves, peace, and quiet. He descended into Oxford Street underground train station.

And emerged in Hyde Park. It was already evening. The sun was going down and the air was cooling. Ogunmola sought out a shaded area and lay down to rest. He dozed off, but sprang awake almost immediately, frightened he might be mugged or something worse could happen. After all, he was in the civilized part of the world. Ogunmola got up and started strolling in the park. Soon he began hearing a voice, which grew louder and louder and was demanding, insisting, stressing. Ogunmola suddenly realized that he was at the famous Hyde Park Corner. He had known about this spot of free public speech even as a kid in secondary school back in Africa, but he had never been curious enough during previous summers in London to want to see it for himself. Now that he had accidentally come upon it, Ogunmola walked resolutely towards the voice.

"...What are we doing here?" the voice was asking. "Thousands of us, or rather, millions of us. There are at least three millions of us, not counting Africans who are citizens of the Americas, spread all over the world. These are three millions of the best sons and daughters of Africa! Now, what are we doing such a crazy thing for? Tell me?"

"You tell us, to begin with, what you are doing here," someone from the sparse audience demanded in an amused tone.

"Sure, I can tell you," he answered eagerly. "I came here to seek knowledge for my own personal benefit and for that of my country. Now, as you can see, this is a very laudable aim, even if my country occupies a secondary place of importance according to my order of priorities. And this is the aim of most of the three millions of us abroad. But there is a catch here, and I want you," the speaker started pointing at a gentleman standing directly in front of him, "I want you to tell us what the catch is. You should know."

"No, why should I know? I'm only a visitor here. So you tell us," the man replied.

"I will. Sure, I will," the speaker resumed. "And it is all very simple. You go out to seek for only that which you do not possess. If you have it, there would be no need to go out in the first place. Now, that means we've come abroad because we're deficient in knowledge and wisdom back home in Africa."

Immediately several voices protested at once.

"You're missing the point, man!"

"Get down, you fool, and stop babbling trash!"

"Listen to me. Listen to me," the speaker pleaded. "I know you'd be outraged at such an atrocious suggestion. But that is the point. We're saying the same thing. So listen to me."

The audience quieted down.

"Of course, it is arrant nonsense to imply, as Westerners out of ignorance once did, that we in Africa were ignorant savages, or that the African world view, when they conceded to the existence of one, was inferior and inadequate. The trouble, however, is that if the best sons and daughters of Africa keep flooding to the West, this can only serve to reinforce the Western man's mistaken notion of innate superiority."

"All that sounds fine," remarked someone from the crowd, "but what do you do about the technology of the Western man? Do you want to pretend we have nothing to learn from him in this respect?"

"That's a good question," the speaker said.

"Then answer it," someone impatiently interrupted.

"I was going to do so," the speaker answered.

"Then do so without stalling," the same impatient voice commanded.

"I am not stalling, and if you would give me a chance, I'd have you understand that Western technology is a must for Africa. Apart from the obvious economic reasons, there are fundamental philosophical and social considerations that make this a must. The priest of *Shango*, for instance, must know the latest concerning the use, control, and generation of electric current, otherwise he would be ignorant of one of the most vital characteristics of the god for whom he ministers. And you know our gods are not dictatorial Western gods who could do whatever they please with humans. On the contrary, our gods owe us, humans, responsibilities. Now, if a *Shango* priest fails to know how to tap electric currents, how would he make his god turn lightning and thunder into the service of humans? How would he help the god fulfil responsibilities to the votaries? And God knows how much we have of those thunders running loose in Africa. So those of you, who thought you had lost your priesthood for going to school, might actually be much more closer to deserving that high office now than ever before."

"Then you're contradicting yourself," jubilantly announced a voice. "You say on one hand that we must go home, and then you turn round to say we need Western technology. How do you explain that?" demanded the voice.

"I am not contradicting myself and I will explain," replied the speaker. "Africa must have the best of Western technology, but there is a myth which must first be destroyed if this is ever going to happen. There is a misconception that going abroad will help us acquire Western technology. As a result, we keep flooding in millions to foreign countries. In our haste, however, we seemed to have overlooked one important fact. We apparently forgot that the kind of technology we need is actually a secret, zealously protected by the owners, and that, in fact, the greatest punishment a nation has, awaits any citizen, found guilty of divulging this secret. So, you see, it is a fallacy to believe that we can come abroad to acquire Western technology. What we are allowed to learn, be it in the classrooms or factories, be it in the East or West, is strictly defined. Why, then, do we rush here in millions, wasting our time? And let me with all honesty point out at this juncture, that we cannot blame these nations for this practice. You cannot, for instance, bring a stranger to your residence and proceed to show him the secrets of your home and of your success. What if the stranger turns round tomorrow to become your enemy and uses his knowledge against you? Therefore, we cannot blame the East or the West for not being foolish. But we must not be foolish either by hoping that they would someday change their attitude. It will never happen."

"What then do you propose?" a man from the audience asked in a tone of genuine concern.

"We must all go home!" the speaker answered emphatically.

"How does isolationism solve the problem?" the same man demanded.

"To begin with," the speaker said, "I am not suggesting that we isolate ourselves. In today's world of fast and efficient communication, even if we want to remain in isolation, we will find it impossible to do so. The latest achievements of science are published in journals on those occasions when such achievements are not classified as national secrets. Anyone can subscribe to these journals and they will be delivered even to the remotest corner of the world. So there will be no isolation. That's not the problem. The problem is that the important achievements of science are usually kept as secrets and we're excluded from sharing them. But we don't have to remain strangers to these secrets. We've been sufficiently exposed to Western technology, and by now we know all the basics. That's all that the West will let us have, and, as a matter of fact, that's all we need to have. The rest depends on us. We have the manpower; we have the resources; what is lacking is the determination to work hard, to persevere, and to make sacrifices in order to acquire our own technological secrets. Until we finally accept the inescapable fact that we cannot eat our cake and have it back, we shall forever continue flooding into Europe and America, and we shall forever keep buying the products of Western technology. This is exactly what the West wants, and this is the reason we must all go home. The sooner the better."

"What are you still doing here then?" jeered somebody.

"To tell you why you must go home," the speaker replied, undaunted. He stepped down from the platform and was immediately surrounded by people seeking to pursue further with him some aspects of the issues he had raised.

Instinctively, Ogunmola also moved in the direction of the speaker because he wanted to know the man's name and to share his own thoughts on the subject with the speaker, but the latter was crowded in. Ogunmola gave up. Instead, he set off for the underground train station, feeling happy he had come to Hyde Park Corner that day. Ogunmola now had a new understanding of his purpose in life. This was what he had always vaguely felt but had been unable to give a name. This was why he had always subconsciously believed that his ancestors were pleased with him without actually understanding the reason for the belief. Ogunmola was glad to realize at last that he was not a blindfolded person trying to lead others. When next he wrote home, he would try to convince his parents no longer to view his educational career as a denial of *Ogun,* but instead as a necessary evil. He would stress the need to update the knowledge about the nature and character of *Ogun* in order both to learn how best to serve the god and to make him fulfil his responsibilities in the most efficient manner to his modern worshippers. No doubt, Ogunmola thought, his studies and later researches would help to illuminate the character of *Ogun* and the role the god had played in the life of his people since the cave age. Besides, wasn't he already carrying out his ministry as it were? Wasn't it *Ogun,* the explorer, the hunter, who had sent him abroad to seek enlightenment which would enable him to minister better to the people? Ogunmola proceeded more confidently and boldly to his London abode. His doubts had been completely resolved. He was happy.

Part Three

The Restoration

The Escalator

Ironically, the more hardships the Nigerian Structural Adjustment Program (SAP) caused fellow citizens, the faster Tinuke lost her anxieties of hunger and gained increasing confidence and assurance that the time for her salvation was at last at hand. When this feeling which was at first elusive became crystallized, it surprised even Tinuke herself that she should be feeling less and less threatened, the more desperate other people became as a result of the mounting difficulties occasioned by SAP. Suddenly one day, the fog of the mystery cleared, and Tinuke began to wonder why, in the first place, such a straightforward affair should have been difficult to understand even for a second. With the lifting of the clouds of mystery, appeared the simple but brilliant plan of action.

After Tinuke and Adisa, her husband, had finalized her travel arrangements, they paid one of their infrequent visits to their family friends, the Olugbengas.

"Well," exclaimed Mr. Olugbenga on seeing the couple. "It has been quite an age," he said. "I thought the gale of SAP had since swept you overseas along with the fortunate ones."

"I guess you're almost right," replied Adisa.

"Now, don't tell me you have only come to say goodbye," said Mr. Olugbenga, genuinely alarmed.

"I'm afraid that's exactly what Tinuke has come to do. She is our John the Baptist. She will prepare the way for the rest of the family to follow later," explained Adisa.

"So you're going abroad!" jubilantly exclaimed Mrs. Olugbenga, coming into the scene from the bedrooms.

"You trust!" boastfully affirmed Tinuke.

The rest of the evening passed with the two couples discussing SAP, which everyone agreed was a national scourge. Details of Tinuke's imminent departure were also analyzed. It emerged that she was heading for Chicago, and at parting, Mrs. Olugbenga, while hugging Tinuke, jovially said: "Well, John the Baptist, make sure you prepare the way for the Olugbengas as well."

* * *

When Tinuke suggested that she be sent ahead to the U.S.A to prepare the way for the rest of the family to later join her, the idea immediately appealed to Adisa. To begin with, the damages of the structural adjustment program, which has the well-deserved acronym SAP, had reached such proportions that anyone who was capable of securing a visa on any pretext whatsoever, got one and ran overseas. Moreover, Tinuke was better placed than her husband, a National Certificate of Education school teacher, to succeed in preparing the grounds for the eventual migration of the whole family. She had a professional training that would sell in the U.S.A.; she had some friends who could minimize the initial hardships of settling illegally in Chicago; above all, her character was made of the stuff to succeed in such circumstances.

Tinuke had a measure of individualism, ambition, and fearlessness that made her look at everything with a certain air of condescension and arrogance. It was as if she already knew that with time she would have everything she wanted, no matter the cost. So why look with reverence at anything that was today beyond reach when all that was required was the courageous determination to wait out the tedium of existence till the golden opportunity presented itself? That this opportunity would present itself sooner than later, she never once entertained a doubt.

Mrs. Olugbenga grew up in the same street as Tinuke and, because this kind of childhood association usually developed deep roots, their friendship had survived the years in spite of periodic problems. Theirs was not what you would call a close friendship; in fact, there were times when they never ran into each other for years, even though they lived in the same town. Nonetheless, there remained a warm depth of feeling between them anytime they met, and also a camaraderie which made them protect each other's interests even at the expense of their husbands.

Thus, for instance, even though Mrs. Olugbenga saw the merit in her husband's criticism of Tinuke, whom he disliked for what he called her crudeness, she was not prepared to betray their friendship. On one occasion, when Tinuke most blatantly abused their friendship by cheating on a business deal, Mrs. Olugbenga nonetheless subtly sabotaged her husband-initiated family decision to terminate her association with Tinuke. Her strategy was at first to keep the friendship on a very low key and to secretly maintain only the most discreet of contacts. Finally, when the right opportunity occurred, she upgraded the relationship to its previous status.

The occasion was the birth of Tinuke's fourth child. Mrs. Olugbenga's argument was that her husband should remember that the new baby was not only Tinuke's but Adisa's as well. Moreover, Mrs. Olugbenga wondered if her husband was so cruel that he could not forgive the past indiscretions of a woman who had already gone through the purifying experience of pregnancy and birth pains. Moreover, to call at this time on Adisa and Tinuke was not to pay a visit on the old sinners, but to welcome a new and innocent arrival to our world.

Before the cultural logic of his wife, Mr. Olugbenga, who respected tradition, had no answer. Moreover, she had touched a soft spot when she hinted that, after all, he had nothing against Adisa in spite of whatever he might hold against the man's wife. Mrs. Olugbenga knew that it was with the greatest reluctance that her husband had severed relationship with Adisa, whose company he had always treasured. Adisa was a world apart from his wife. He was so intelligent and knowledgeable, yet so unassuming and humble. His company was always a pleasure to Mr. Olugbenga, largely because Adisa, though determinedly involved in the daily efforts for survival, seemed completely removed from the ugly side of this struggle in a society that was viciously materialistic. There was a quiet, unobtrusive feeling of self-confidence and completeness in Adisa which made him pleasant and acceptable to everyone. Mr. Olugbenga always secretly admired Adisa's simplicity and the infinite patience that almost made him look like a holy fool. But then, as Mr. Olugbenga would frequently admit, one had to have infinite patience to live with a wife like Tinuke. To Mr. Olugbenga, Tinuke was the height of crude arrogance and selfish individualism. Nonetheless, his repulsion faded into the background before the anticipated pleasure of Adisa's company and before the agreeable, cultural duty of welcoming a newly born.

* * *

This was how it came about that, after a couple of years of having severed contacts, the Olugbengas visited Adisa and Tinuke and thus resurrected a shaken friendship. In spite of Tinuke's irrepressibly unpleasant personality, this friendship survived the years following the renewal of contacts. The magic was in Mrs. Olugbenga's diplomacy, Mr. Olugbenga's forbearance, and Adisa's pleasant personality.

Three years after Tinuke left for Chicago, the Olugbengas also fled the pains of SAP by going to the United States. By then, they had completely lost touch with Tinuke who was also most irregular in writing to her husband. The last time Mr. Olugbenga saw Adisa, the latter bitterly complained that he had not heard from his wife for several months running: "After I had supplied all the documents she needed for college admission and visa normalization," he said, "her letters suddenly stopped coming. And if only you knew what I suffered going to offices located at different corners of the state to obtain those documents!" complained Adisa. "And now, she does not as much as send even a card!" Adisa was disappointed and worried. "Perhaps she is sick or in some trouble." Adisa looked completely perplexed.

"I do not think you need to worry. She will be all right, you'll see," Mr. Olugbenga said, trying to cheer him up.

Several months after this chance encounter in a street in Ibadan, the Olugbengas left for the United States of America, with Adisa pleading that they should try locating his wife and send word. Barely six months after the Olugbengas had settled in the United States, Mr. Olugbenga had reasons to take a trip home. He flew into New York and, while he was reading some newspapers during the wait to board his flight, a familiar voice called his name. He looked up and to his surprise saw Adisa standing before him, all clothed in black. He had the defeated look of one newly bereaved.

"How come you're here? What happened?" Mr. Olugbenga asked in succession.

"I came to the States shortly after you left, and I'm going back to bury my father."

"I'm awfully sorry. When did this happen?" Mr. Olugbenga was relieved, for his fears had concerned some other person.

"About a week now," Adisa replied. "I wasn't too surprised though. He was seventy eight and had been sick, but I had hoped that he would survive till Christmas."

"I'm sorry," Mr. Olugbenga condoled again. "How is Tinuke?"

"I guess she is alright," Adisa said in a tellingly tired voice.

"What do you mean?" Olugbenga asked.

"Well," Adisa drawled out in a supremely tired voice, "that's another story altogether, but right now, I'm concerned about arranging the burial of my father. I'm his first child and his only son."

"I'm terribly sorry," Mr. Olugbenga sympathized once more.

* * *

Nonetheless, during the flight, Adisa told Mr. Olugbenga this other story concerning Tinuke. Having failed to receive any communication from Tinuke, Adisa had decided to carry out his already delayed plan of going to the United States of America on his own without the planned help of his wife. He obtained study leave from his teaching post, sold his last plot of land, put the children in the care of his father-in-law, and left for America on a visiting visa. On getting to Chicago, he started making telephone inquiries to track down his wife. To his amazement, those who should know claimed that they were ignorant of her whereabouts. Others who seemed to know, were most reluctant, as if they didn't think it was proper to disclose her address. Some, for reasons of their own, preferred to laugh, as if his inquiry was a joking matter. After their mysterious laughter, they quickly changed the topic to other things. How were people back home surviving SAP? What were the politicians up to? Were the military boys really serious about returning the country to civilian rule? As if he had come all the way from Nigeria to stay at an airport telephone booth to discuss Nigerian politics! Finally, Adisa got a lead that took him to his wife's door.

"What are you doing here?" was her welcome when she opened

her door to discover him. He had the feeling that she might not have opened the door if she had known it was he ringing the bell. Nonetheless, he was reluctantly admitted into her apartment and, thereafter, everything went as strangely as his reception.

"Well, I discovered soon enough that I could no longer lay claims on her as a husband. I was just being tolerated and she made me understand that I had better find my way out of her apartment and out of her life as quickly as possible. I graduated from amazement to anger and when anger made things even worse, I went into a temporary limbo of confusion, anger, and more confusion. After a while, I reconciled myself to the bitter reality and, because of the children, I condescended to making appeals to her sense of traditional beliefs, the claims of family, her sense of morality and the simple injustice of ditching me after I had done so much, including incurring yet unpaid debts, to get her to America.

"All this failed to move her. I even got her relatives back home to write, phone, and appeal to her, but all to no avail. In fact, the appeals seemed only to infuriate her and make her determined to be even more nasty to me. She rarely was in the apartment, and any time she was there, it was continuous high tension. So, in fact, I was glad when she was away, but the tension of her presence was replaced with the loneliness of her absence.

"It was in this state, which lasted four months, that I received the message of the death of my father. She was as usual not in the apartment. I had not seen or spoken with her for over a month, and this was when she last visited the apartment to warn me to move out. Friends were already tired, advising me to quit her place, forget about her, and set out on a fresh new life of my own. But the thought of the children kept me there, hoping against hope that Tinuke would see reason sooner or later and that our lives would be back together on the old path of joint hope and aspiration.

"I found it hard to believe that everything had collapsed, that I had to start all over again, and at this age! In a way, my father's death was a welcome relief for bringing an end to the impasse. It had been a harrowing time and I'm glad I have survived it even though I'm badly battered. Truly, I'm glad that I'm alive to bury my father even if I'm yet to know how I'll manage to obtain the resources and energy to do it. I feel completely sapped of all energy. I'm tired, very tired." Adisa was sad and he looked twice his forty-eight years.

"I'm sorry, really sorry you had to go through all this," consoled

Mr. Olugbenga.

Suddenly Adisa started chuckling and heaving uncontrollably with humor. Finally, he controlled himself and while still shaking with laughter, he rhetorically asked Mr. Olugbenga: "Do you know how Tinuke, my wife, bade me goodbye?"

"How?" asked Mr. Olugbenga.

"Somehow she got wind of my bereavement and of my plan to travel, so she timed her coming to the apartment today in the morning to within minutes of my departure. Without even as much as a pretence at condolence, and using the most deliberate and emphatic voice she could command, she said to me: 'Make sure you take along with you every single thing in this apartment that belongs to you, even a pin. Anything you leave behind will go to the garbage heap. And don't you ever let me see your face again.' That was how she bade me farewell."

"That was most cruel," Mr. Olugbenga remarked.

"No, it was good she did; those words were like a magical wand. They cleared any illusions I might have been harboring. The more I look at it, the more I realize now that my father's death is truly a blessing. You might find this hard to believe, but the truth is that Tinuke now seems to have happened millions of years ago."

"I'm glad for you," Mr. Olugbenga said, relieved.

* * *

When on arriving home Mr. Olugbenga narrated the story of Adisa, his brother-in-law, who grew up with Tinuke in the same street, observed that it was all the fault of Adisa. "If he had not married her," the brother-in-law said, "she would have remained an eternal spinster. She was the ugliest girl in town. What did he see in her?" the brother-in-law wondered. "And on top of it all, he would incur debts to send her ahead to the U.S.A. instead of going himself. Serves him right!"

* * *

When Adisa left Tinuke's apartment for the airport, Tinuke actually went about the rooms collecting bits and pieces left by him. She tied them in a garbage bag which she took outside and deposited in the garbage bin. She returned to the apartment, vacuumed it, and started a thorough general clean-up to remove the minutest trace of her husband and the past. She completed the job in under an hour because the husband had always been a neat person. On completing the relatively easy task, she heaved a monumental sight of relief, and settled into a chair with a cup of coffee and a doughnut.

Life, she was thinking, had been most unfair to her. She had lost her mother before school-age, and had been brought up by a harsh step-mother. Nature had been most spiteful. In a country where women were already underprivileged, she, a woman, was born with distinctively unattractive features: a short, fat, and broad body, pitch dark complexion, fat ugly calves, manly voice, and a wide, unpretty face. Quite early in life, she had decided to fight nature's spitefulness. If it was nature's intention to consign her to the fringe of society, she resolved to show nature that she too had a say in the matter by fighting her way right back to the front row. However, it seemed that nature was equally determined to frustrate her efforts. The easiest way for people to push their way out of obscurity at that time was to excel in educational endeavors, but she was no good in school work. She ended up at a catering school regarded by many inhabitants as the dumping ground of academic failures, but she soon grew to like it because the cover-all uniform provided a good camouflage for her fat and short ugly shape. Moreover, men were forever parading before their hostels, and she hoped to use all the tricks in the feminine book to try to attract attention to herself. But all the attention she got was from men who had come to the hostel to discover that their dates had jilted them, and even these men very quickly discarded her, after using her to assuage their temporary hurt.

She managed in the end, after repeating a number of courses, to secure a certificate. She had been working as a caterer in a hotel in Ibadan for five years and had resigned herself to life as an eternal spinster when Adisa came along. He was not a particularly attractive man himself, but he was by all accounts a good catch. He held an NCE certificate, was already employed as a teacher in a secondary school where his prospects were good, and he seemed extremely patient and sympathetic. Something even told her that the attention he paid her was out of sympathy. Even though she resented this, she had no other choice; so, when Adisa showed interest beyond the first dates, she quickly adopted a strategy to get him to propose. And he proposed. She hastened the wedding to make sure he had no time to change his mind. But he was not even planning to change his mind, and she discovered this fact long after the wedding, when the first child, whose conception she had also hastened, was well on his way.

The discovery further humiliated her and she became even more acutely aware of her physical limitations. However, she resolved more firmly than ever before to ride over those limitations. She was going to show everybody by her actions that she was in no way inferior to anyone. She started flaunting the fact of her marriage, particularly before those who had said openly to her face or those she knew had thought it in their minds—and these included almost all her acquaintances—that she would never get a man to marry her. She flaunted her children, and also wore her work uniforms and outing dresses as if they became her, and as if she were a beauty. She used their one car as if it were only one of many they owned. She hurried her husband to build a house as a show of success, and spoke condescendingly of other peoples' successes and achievements as if they were incomparable with what she had achieved or was about to achieve.

However, in spite of the outward show, she was deeply unhappy inside. She hated it because she often suspected that people saw through her. She hated what she had to go through in order to get the money to maintain her charade. She often walked rough-shod in monetary matters over even her few genuine friends. She was forever taking advantage of her husband and, because the husband rarely complained, she developed a guilt-feeling which imperceptibly evolved into a dislike for him. While she was forever scheming on advancing her own personal interests, the husband always blindly believed her when she presented those interests as those of the family. This was how he docilely agreed to her suggestion to meet the hardships of economic depression by setting her up in trading. He went and borrowed money and she started going first to Lagos on weekends and then on working days whenever she could buy sick-leave, in order to purchase products to retail in Ibadan. Later, she convinced the husband to loan more money to sponsor summer trading trips to Italy.

It was during her first trip to Rome that she became convinced that she had been born in the wrong part of the world. The anonymity of the individual in the white man's world, the orderly organization of life, the abundance of all sorts of facilities, and the unlimited opportunities for self-realization which she saw there convinced her that she had no alternative but to transfer to where she was convinced was the right part of the world. At this time, the economic situation in Nigeria had drastically deteriorated as a result of the introduction of what everyone agreed was appropriately called SAP. The weird logic of this economic program seemed to be that to restore life to the dying economy, every juice had first to be SAPped out of the underprivileged majority citizens. The middle class rapidly disappeared, and the garbage heaps of the increasingly rich few became the food table of the multiplied population of abjectly poor. Brain-drain to the oil-rich Arab countries and to the Western world became a flood. The worse the situation got, the more confident Tinuke became of realizing her aspiration. All she needed as usual was to select the appropriate time to represent to her husband her own personal goal as that of the family and, as always, she was sure he would approve whatever project she proposed for the realization of the identified goal.

This was how the plan to send her ahead to Chicago, which she learned was a more prosperous place than Rome, was born. She worked feverishly for a quick realization of this plan which she knew would mark the end of the hated past and the beginning of a new life, unencumbered in any way by remnants of the past. She would have a clean break. This was the spirit in which she bade goodbye to husband, children, relatives, and friends who had no suspicion that she did not plan to ever see them again. However, instead of the immediate and complete break she had planned by severing all contacts, she discovered to her chagrin on arriving in Chicago that she needed to write her husband to supply all manners of documents she needed to start her new life. But after all the documents had been obtained, she effectively cut all communication.

So when Adisa without warning materialized at her door just over three years after she had settled in Chicago, she was greatly angered. She thought of slamming the door in his face, but thought the better of it and admitted him. But no sooner had he entered than she began to make it clear to him that he was an unwelcome stranger.

After the initial rough, very rough, introduction to Chicago life, she had soon found her feet. It was amazing to even herself how so quickly she forgot about all she had left behind in Nigeria. At the time of Adisa's rude intrusion, she already had a completely new life smoothly running to its rhythm, oiled by the American efficiency and sufficiency. Adisa appeared to her to be so old and so remote she could not understand his language which expressed strange notions of responsibility and morality, and staked claims to some affinity. Somehow, she understood there was a need to provide this stranger some money, space, and time to settle himself in a world in which he was clearly a disadvantaged arrival. She disappeared after that to reappear periodically from the sanctuary of her lover's home to remind Adisa, the apparition from the past, of the time he had left to vacate her apartment. He seemed impervious to her warnings because, apparently, his legendary patience had made him believe that with time, she, Mary Jones who used to be called Tinuke, would understand his language again. Mary Jones was, in fact, at the point of forcefully ejecting him when his father's death mercifully intervened.

Professor's Focal Adjustment

Dr. Bamidele, a full professor of literature at the City University of Lagos, closed his office door at four o'clock and started walking home. A partially damaged umbrella was in one hand, and in the other a leather bag containing books and student scripts. He had lately exhumed the bag from under heaps of books and old clothes in the study closet. It was the bag he had used as a student in London and it was worn and old and that was the reason he had discarded it when he started teaching fifteen years before. It was certainly not befitting, going around as a lecturer with that sort of bag, but for sentimental reasons and because the bag still held well in spite of age, he did not throw it away. He saved some papers in it and kept it in the study. In fact, he had forgotten that the bag still existed until recently when the fashionable Samsonite he acquired as a lecturer became so old it was a shame to be seen with it. He was complaining he could not afford the SAP-induced inflated price of a new bag and was wondering what to do, when his wife assured him there must be some usable bag somewhere in the house and that he should search well for it.

This was how he rediscovered his student bag. He was fully conscious of the irony of returning as a professor to a book bag he had thought disgraceful for a lecturer. He had also observed on a number of occasions how his students secretly made jest of him on account of the bag. In spite of this embarrassment, he had to keep using it, if he did not want the rains to spoil his books and student scripts. At the price for which books were currently selling, it was impossible to think of replacing a damaged book. In fact, he had been unable to purchase any new books since the Structural Adjustment Program (SAP) became fully operational. If it were the time his Peugeot was drivable, he would simply have carried the books and scripts by hand and dumped them on the car seat, but it was past a month since his car had broken down.

At the time the car first developed trouble, his mechanic had told him he needed only three hundred naira to put it back on the road. Unfortunately, it was the second week of the month and he had only on the previous day obtained an overdraft to feed the family for the rest of the month. His policy used to be never be indebted to anybody or any institution, except in the case of major purchases like buying a car or a house which were beyond the means of any ordinary university teacher to pay for in cash and in full. Frugal family beginnings, morally strong Catholic education, a Spartan university life, and the reality of the sociopolitical and economic environment had taught him to hold firmly to the philosophy of living exclusively within his means. He had no excesses: didn't smoke, drink or womanize, had few friends, and was not a member of any social club. He lived with his wife and two children, a boy and a girl aged ten and twelve, almost as a recluse, and concentrated on providing the needs of his immediate family and as much as possible of the extended relations. He spent also on the essential tools for advancement in his profession: books, journals, and conferences.

Until 1986, when SAP fully came into effect, Dr. Bamidele had been able to do all these things without borrowing, although it had become increasingly difficult each successive year. By 1987, after he had cut expenses on the extended family and on items like books, journals, and conferences, which sadly by then had become unaffordable luxuries, it was still impossible to meet the essential needs of his immediate family without borrowing. At first he had found it difficult and shameful to approach his Bank Manager, but necessity soon gave him the courage and taught him the language to negotiate for bank overdrafts. This, in fact, had become the reality of his life for the past two years; the only difference was that his salary used to last for three weeks in 1987 whereas in 1988 he could stretch it for only two weeks, despite the fact that all luxuries such as egg, chicken, beef, rice, bread, milk, coffee, tea, and beverages rarely appeared on the family's dining table any more. Previously despised foods like beans, frozen fish, roasted groundnut, cooked or roasted corn, which they rarely tasted in the past, had now become their staple diet along with the common *garri* and yam which used to be the poor man's food but which have recently graduated in status through inflated pricing. It had been a long time since the family bought any new clothes and shoes. While Dr. Bamidele and his wife could manage somehow, it was a matter of daily shame and pain watching their children force themselves into outworn and outgrown clothes and shoes. But no matter the extent of their pain and shame with regard to clothing, all that Dr. Bamidele's professorial salary, assisted by a monthly overdraft, could barely achieve was providing food, medicine, housing, school fees, and transportation.

Dr. Bamidele had always believed in keeping his car in good condition. He feared intercity public transportation because of excessive speeding and frequent fatal road accidents, and he disliked intracity transportation because it was dirty, chaotic, inadequate, and unreliable. Moreover, one would be helpless should there be an emergency in the night. Even in the days before SAP, the telephone could not be counted upon to work nor was the ambulance service of even private institutions, let alone those of government hospitals, always reliable. In the case of police emergency, the usual reply was for the station officer to complain that there was no vehicle to bring help. In the era of SAP, with the markedly increased undernourishment of children and frequency of sickness, with the prevalence of fake drugs, fake spare car parts, and increased instances of road accidents and crime, owning a functional car had become a nonnegotiable necessity for Dr. Bamidele. But he had been forced to do without this necessity for the past month.

The day after the car had broken down, Dr. Bamidele went to his Bank Manager to ask for a loan of three hundred naira that was required for its repair, but the manager had refused to grant the loan.

"Prof.," the manager had respectfully begun, "please try to understand me. I do sympathize with your situation, but you have to know that I am permitted to give only loans which can be realistically repaid. Already, half of your salary goes into repaying monthly overdrafts approved to enable you feed the family. This, you know, is a great concession that we granted you because of your social status and excellent character. It is a favor many people, including several of your colleagues who have been denied, would be happy to get in this Bank. With the daily increase in inflation, I cannot see how you can repay any additional loan since all you have is your salary. You must forgive me, Prof., but I have to remind you that the Bank is not a philanthropic institution."

After he was dismissed from the manager's office, Dr. Bamidele did not know where to hide his face out of shame, disappointment, and frustration. He felt completely helpless and powerless and was blindly walking out of the premises of the Bank, thinking of how to get transportation back to the campus where he lived in university quarters, when a senior colleague called his name. The colleague wanted to remind him of how crucial it was for Dr. Bamidele to attend the senate committee meeting scheduled for the next day to discuss academic job rationalization. He could not care less for any committee meeting at that point, but he was glad to learn that he could catch a ride with his colleague who was heading back to the quarters where he too lived.

"It seems the government is determined to destroy the university system completely," remarked Dr. Bamidele's colleague as they were driving back to the campus. "It does not bother government that we no longer have the means to carry out our basic academic functions of teaching and research, instead government is bent on further frustrating us by threatening our jobs with rationalization measures. Dr. Bamidele, you must be sure to attend the meeting tomorrow. We need to make government realize that it cannot humiliate us any further than it already has."

Although Dr. Bamidele equally strongly detested the sinister motives of the rationalization plan, he was not in the mood to discuss the issue nor was he interested in attending the committee meeting planned for the next day. His recent experience at the Bank was still heavily weighing on him. Moreover, he was convinced that little would be achieved by the isolated voices of isolated universities protesting negative government measures. Only the united voice of all the universities backed by a concerted labor action was capable of effecting any significant change and this voice, he regretted, had been effectively silenced by a government ban order. He noted the irony that the colleague giving him a ride, and who was belatedly arguing for a voice against government's evil plans, was one of those who had enthusiastically hailed the ban on their union when it was imposed. At the time, this colleague and the professors and lecturers in his camp had argued that the union was too radical and confrontational to government and that it was right for it to be banned. Dr. Bamidele had belonged to the camp supporting the union, which had insisted with reasoned argument, supported by hard evidence from other nations' experience, that the Structural Adjustment Program (SAP) planned by the government would inevitably produce spiral inflation, massive unemployment, mass poverty, a new wave of crime, premature deaths, and brain-drain. Now that these predictions as well as others which had warned of the corrupt acquisition of public property by a few through privatization, the destruction of the middle class, the undermining of the educational system, particularly the university and tertiary institutions, had come true, his colleague and others in his camp had suddenly grown wise. Dr. Bamidele did not want to pretend he approved of his colleague's politics, so he made a token statement and changed the topic.

"Well, you seem to be forgetting that the position of the government and its advisers is that tertiary education, especially the university, is dispensable. In any case, tell me, is it true that harsher conditions are to be imposed on academic promotions as of this session?"

"It is indeed true," the colleague confirmed. "Do you mean you have not received the memo on this subject? It was distributed early last week."

"I don't read memos anymore," disclosed Dr. Bamidele. "They only aggravate the blood pressure. But tell me, how more sickly can this our university get? Not only has it selected to further depress the morale of an already SAP-demoralized community, it has turned its back completely on logic and morality. I learned that henceforth, while associate professors will wait only two years for promotion, assistant lecturers who are just starting their careers and are the least paid, will have to wait five or more years to be considered for promotion. What kind of logic is that, tell me!"

"It is sad," commented Dr. Bamidele's colleague, "but the explanation I have heard is economically logical, for the measure is the administration's response to budget cuts. Since junior academics are larger in number, the university hopes to save money by implementing the plan."

"Well, let's wait and see how many junior academics will remain here next year," remarked Dr. Bamidele. "This isn't the only university in the country. No doubt, the understaffed state universities will be glad to learn that we are preparing to convert ours into a recruitment ground for them. In any case, since the professors who in all probability suggested the plan in the first place are being so well pampered, they should be well prepared for heavier teaching loads."

"Don't forget you're a professor too," Dr. Bamidele's colleague reminded him. "Are you stopping here in the faculty or going straight to your quarters?"

Dr. Bamidele elected to go first to his office. He thanked his colleague and alighted in front of the faculty buildings, which once looked imposing but now looked at everyone with the reproving sadness of premature aging and neglect; a look that was duplicated in the faces of the hungry and demoralized students and professors who no longer had research or conference funds, and who taught without books, journals, and basic classroom and laboratory supplies. Dr. Bamidele walked to his office, where he had nothing to do because he needed time to compose himself before going home to face his wife with the news of his failure to secure a loan to repair their car.

Dr. Bamidele had held tenaciously to the belief that he was a success as far as his profession went and, as evidence, he was always quick to point out that he was not some political, "*son-of-the-soil*" professor, but one highly regarded both locally and internationally. However, in sombre moments like this, he could not help accepting the verdict of his wife who saw him as a social failure. While respecting his professional success, his wife remained a clear-eyed realist who insisted that a man who could not feed his family had no right considering himself successful. His argument that her judgment had ignored the unusual circumstances of the times was countered, like the realist she was, by the claim that unusual circumstances demanded unusual resolutions.

Some of Dr. Bamidele's colleagues had in fact taken one or other of what his wife referred to as unusual resolutions and were coping successfully with SAP. His wife had agreed with him that it was dishonest earning a regular salary as an academic while in actual fact one spent the greater percentage of one's time in the business world negotiating contracts as some of his colleagues were doing at the time. She also agreed with him that it was degrading to snuggle up to the authorities with the intention of securing preferential treatment and rewards in the form of university appointments or board membership in government companies, or a cozy ministerial post. She similarly agreed with him that there was no sense in taking on too many academic obligations such as, for instance, serving as an external examiner or doing part-time teaching, when all the money earned from these exhausting activities did little to tilt the balance of SAP inflation in one's favor. They knew of a neighbor who spent more money than he had earned nursing himself back to health after breaking down from over-stretching himself doing part-time teaching at a university in a neighboring State. While Dr. Bamidele's wife did not want the futility of honest, academic over-laboring, nor the dishonesty of academic businessmen, nor the immorality of academic prostitutes despite the cozy rewards, she was quite prepared for whatever inconveniences voluntary exile overseas would entail. In any case, this was the option already chosen by the majority of the academically sound among her husband's colleagues.

"Even though you're not a medical doctor and cannot go to Saudi Arabia to earn a fat salary," she said to her husband, "you can at least earn enough money abroad to feed, clothe, and house us. But you refuse to try. And it is not as if you were an academic deadwood who could never secure a position in Britain or America, but you just will not try! Obviously, you consider yourself a greater patriot than those who have wisely fled overseas."

These were her bitter remarks the last time they had discussed their situation. When he vehemently denied the accusation of a holier-than-you patriot, she came heavily down on him and accused him of psychological morbidity.

"Then you must be secretly in love with poverty in spite of your loud protestations to the contrary. Or you enjoy the sense of constant danger," she further accused him and then added: "For your information, though, and in case you've not yet noticed, my nerves are already at the point of completely breaking down for having been constantly on edge for far too long. I want a place where I can go to sleep at night without the eternal fear of being awakened by armed robbers. I want to be able to drive on the roads without being afraid that my car can be snatched at gunpoint. I want to be able to know that if I fall sick, I will not be going to a hospital already completely emptied of their best doctors or where I could be treated with fake drugs. I want also to be freed of the fear of fake motor spare parts causing fatal road accidents. I no longer want to be tortured by fear every time I go to the market, scared that I may be as unfortunate as the women who had wiped out the entire members of their families and them-selves, eating death-carrying *garri*, which they had bought from igno-rant and avaricious businessmen turned emergency processors of arsenic foods. Even if you have no pity for yourself or for me, can't you see that your children are drying up? Can't you see the faded, out-grown clothes into which they daily force themselves?"

She had wanted to say more, but restrained herself because she loved her husband and did not want to hurt his feelings too deeply. After all, she knew that he genuinely cared for the family and all that she herself really wanted was to pressurize him into overcoming his reluctance to take what under the circumstances seemed to her the only rational decision left for him. Dr. Bamidele also knew what his wife was up to and even though he was irritated, he was not angry. He was only disappointed she had not chosen to discuss the matter in a more rational manner. Although the wife regretted her outburst, she was nonetheless pleased that she had succeeded in forcefully making her point. She knew that her husband would have been less moved if she had been more calm and rational.

At the earliest opportunity following his wife's outburst and at every suitable occasion thereafter, Dr. Bamidele had repeatedly explained his own stand. First of all, he said that he was tired of being a rootless plant without a home. He believed that it was all well and enriching to have stayed several years abroad as he did while a stu-dent in Britain, but now he was no longer a young man, and at his present age he had looked forward to an established life in familiar surroundings. He observed that at that moment, he was just still try-ing to deal with the bitter disappointment that at the very point in his life when he was actually beginning to establish solid roots, the Structural Adjustment Program had come along like a senseless child to destroy the edifice of several years of careful labor as if it were only a sand castle. He had worked so hard at achieving professional suc-cess and it was just when he had arrived there and everything should begin to fall into place, that he suddenly woke up to find SAP sadis-tically jeering at his years of efforts and self-denial. Just when he had begun to congratulate himself for running a good race and was antic-ipating a well-deserved rest and reward, he discovered that the race has been frivolously nullified by the mindless umpire SAP. This was the disappointment he was still trying to deal with, the disappoint-ment of a total failure, without a roof which he could call his own, without a *kobo* in his Bank account. The disappointment in the jeering emptiness of an unsecured future, the inability even to feed himself and his family and provide the daily necessities of life. He was still feeling so completely cheated by and angry with the elements in the society who had created the monster-child SAP that he was still finding it difficult to start contemplating the possibility of once more uprooting himself to start life all over again in the rough and only half-familiar terrain of Britain or America.

"And don't underestimate the hardships of that terrain in spite of its present allurement," he warned his wife. "It might seem illogical now, but believe me, you will be longing to be reunited to this life-denying and SAPped country in only a couple of years. And this homesickness will be accentuated each time any citizen of the host country whose tax money and ancestral blood had built the amenities you're going to be enjoying, makes you realize, however subtly, that you're only a tolerated, sponging stranger. There are even a few who by action and word will pointedly tell you on racist grounds, to go home if you do not like being patronized or treated like a subhuman species or a 'glorified slave' as, you will recall, our doctor friend said in his last letter to us from an Arab capital. As for the children, have you bothered to think of what future awaits them if we flee abroad?" he had asked his wife. "What sort of allegiance do you think they will owe to this land which they are forced to abandon because it cannot feed or protect them? What cultural identity will they have? They could never be British or American because they are not, and they will never be fully accepted as one however much they try to integrate. Yet they will be ashamed of a home whose only memory is of hunger, deprivations, and insecurity. At that point will the children bless or curse us?"

Dr. Bamidele went on to explain to his wife that despite the fact that there was much to be ashamed of in their ravaged country, there still existed positive qualities that uniquely defined them as a people, which he wished his children to grow up to identify with, acquire and cherish. "It is well and good," he stressed, "for people with strong national roots to claim to be floating world citizens. They have in reserve and beneath their probably serious claims the reassuring feeling of a home with which they subconsciously identify. I do not know how truly happy those who have no such psychological reservoir will be, claiming international citizenship in a world where everyone they meet waves a flag of national identity. Do we want to deprive our children of this sense of identity?"

Dr. Bamidele further discussed his reluctance to go abroad by explaining its implication for his profession, his feeling of nationalism, and his sense of fulfillment. "You see," he had told his wife, "literature, my subject, is taught everywhere in the world with a national bias. This is not ideal, but it is natural, and it is unfortunately the reality we have to deal with until the world is more united. For several years now, I have identified my purpose of existence with teaching literature in a way to make the Nigerian student a better Nigerian citizen. And remember, only a good Nigerian can be a good world citizen. I have seen this as my major contribution to nation-building and the most significant validation of my existence. I put all my energy into this process of validation, and because I know I am doing the right thing, and also because I achieve results and I know from positive responses that I am appreciated, I feel enormously happy doing it. It fulfils me. Now, when I get to Britain or Saudi Arabia, how will I get fulfillment? According to the theory of Democracy, I should be serving a useful purpose by using literature to broaden the cultural horizon of the British or the Saudi student, but even in the most tolerant Democracy, there is a difference between theory and practice. It is one thing, for instance, for the American professor to be democratic in an American lecture room and quite another thing for a Nigerian professor to be democratic in the same classroom. Therefore, to remain a welcome guest abroad, I shall have to learn to deal with my new environment. I am still figuring out how I am going to do this and until I have worked it out, it will be premature for me to go overseas."

These discussions had gone on for several months before Dr. Bamidele's car broke down, and it was not until his futile trip to his Bank that he finally reconciled himself to the inevitable. His resolution, taken late in the evening in his office where his colleague had dropped him in the afternoon, gave him courage to leave the office and go home to meet his wife and children. But even as he announced his intention and read his first letters of application to British universities to his wife, he still could not help expressing his reluctance: "Although it is futile and even stupid to remain here since we have responsibilities to the children and neither of us has the heroism to compel the change of the SAP policy," he began to explain, "nonetheless, I cannot shake off the feeling of shame that I am abandoning my country like a sinking ship without doing all within my ability to rescue it."

He conceded the possibility that his metaphor of the sinking ship, as government supporters strenuously argued, might be vastly exaggerated, but he could not shake off the shameful feeling of a deserter even as he daily increased the number of job applications he sent to Britain. The hope that he and his wife might somehow succeed in scraping money together to put their car back on the road was finally dashed at the end of the month when the mechanic informed him that, as a result of recent astronomical increases in the prices of spare motor parts, he would now need close to a thousand naira to do the old job. The estimates given by other mechanics whom he consulted were even higher. Dr. Bamidele's reaction to this development was to intensify his search for a job overseas.

That afternoon at four o'clock, when Dr. Bamidele closed his office door and started walking home with a torn umbrella in one hand and a worn student bag in another, it was already past a month since he started flooding Britain with job applications. The new difficulty of going to work, walking the children to school, and visiting town to obtain provisions from the local markets without a car, further fueled the determination to escape SAP as quickly as possible now that the decision to go abroad has been irrevocably taken.

Absorbed in thought as he walked home, Dr. Bamidele nearly got run over by a car at the last intersection before his staff quarters. When he got home, everybody was wearing a blooming smile as if SAP were already a thing of the past, and as if what they ate for lunch had not been only roasted groundnuts and boiled corn, a meal his children had christened "kwashiorkor." Dr. Bamidele assumed that the smile had something to do with the fact that his wife had somehow managed to scrape money together to cook the family's favorite dish for dinner. In fact, he was savoring the aroma of chicken in *egusi* and *ewuro* soup for pounded yam which was floating from the kitchen as he sat down in the sitting room sofa to undo his shoes, when everybody in unison shouted *SURPRISE!* He turned to see his daughter produce a DHL courier package. He didn't have to be told what message it contained. He heaved a monumental sigh of relief, but, amidst all his joys, he was fully conscious that the package was also the signal of the beginning of an unwanted, though necessary, fundamental adjustment in the direction and substance of their lives. That night he cried in his sleep for himself and family, particularly for the children.

Permutations of
Triple Zero

The middle-aged Political Science senior lecturer, popularly known by students as *the Guy* because of his love for American slang and clothing, stood slim and fit in front of the third-year students of the City University of Lagos, lecturing on the theoretic root, practical dimensions, and international political significance of *perestroika:*

"The surprise is not that *perestroika,* which figuratively can be seen as the last nail on the coffin of communism, has finally been driven in," he began, "but that it took so long for this nail to be driven in. The present demise of communism, the Great Evil, was already evident at its birth for, as well informed political scientists have been observing from the beginning, it was a political ideology that was as moribund in theory as it was impracticable in reality. Let me elaborate...."

And he went on to elaborate most exhaustively and with the relish of a lecturer who obviously loved his topic. Then he paused and asked: "Any questions?" After an embarrassing silence when no student indicated interest by a raise of the hand, he repeated: "Any questions?" His request was repeated a third time as the students continued to maintain silence, unsure if it was safe to raise questions which challenged the views that he had expressed in a manner which left no one in doubt that they were his articles of faith. He was going to proceed to further elaborations and new points when at last a hand timorously crawled up, indicating a readiness to ask questions. "Yes, can we have your question?" the lecturer encouraged.

"I was wondering, Sir," the student hesitantly began, "if there was any difference between communism and socialism. I'm asking because a book I read said there were as yet no communist countries, only socialist countries aspiring to communism. Secondly, Sir, the explanation of *perestroika* that I have come across suggests that it is an attempt to purify socialist practice of its Stalinist impurities. In other words, Sir, *perestroika* from this perspective is a new socialist beginning. And finally, Sir, what implications has all this for the theory of African Socialism as propounded by leaders like Julius Nyerere and Amical Cabral?"

"Apparently," the lecturer's answer began, "you have been listening too much to apologists of communism who would want to bamboozle you with nonexisting distinctions. Take it from me, buddy, that socialism and communism are names for the same disease whose symptoms became evident thanks to Stalin. And as for your African Socialism, it has, fortunately, been buried in the same coffin with its Eastern father by *perestroika*."

"Is it then true, Sir," a second student boldly began to ask before seeking permission, "that man's dream for equality has irretrievably been buried with this *perestroika* of a coffin?"

The class burst out into a hilarious uproar which infected the lecturer himself who could not help but join in the laughter. When the noise had subsided, the lecturer's reply provoked yet another round of laughter and cheerfulness: "I'm a political scientist performing a postmortem on a twentieth century theoretic corpse, and not a futurologist prognosticating on when the fingers of the hands will be of equal length. Got it, fellow?" The lecturer pronounced the last word "*fella*," and he was smiling, amused by his own cleverness.

A note of seriousness was reintroduced into the discussion by a third student.

"If your statement is right, Sir, it means that there is no alternative to capitalism and that since we are the unequal fingers in this capitalist hand, it also means that we are forever doomed to suffer exploitation as we've done before and are currently doing under the capitalist agenda of Structural Adjustment Program (SAP)."

At this point, a student once again introduced a note of lightheartedness by an interjection that sent the class reeling in laughter. He said: "In that case, we might as well all give up on this side of the globe and ask *perestroika* to nail us inside the communist coffin."

"Class!" the lecturer called in a serious tone with an underlying threat that sought to reestablish his authority. "Class," he ominously called again, "I think we had better be serious." After a brief silence which he purposely allowed to ensue in order to further emphasize his authority, he continued to speak. "It is pretty clear at this stage—and I do not believe it has ever been in any serious doubt—that capitalism is the better political and economic system. And as for SAP, it is a necessary bitter pill to keep us healthy in the happy family of capitalism."

"I beg to seriously disagree with you here, Sir," a student boldly interrupted. "SAP is certainly not a medicine for health but a subtle road to enslavement. And it is an enslavement, Sir, that is worse than the 18th century slavery. Look at it this way, Sir: In the 18th century, only a portion of our population was physically enslaved, but now all of the population is enslaved. It was not enough that they dictated the price we paid for both what we sold and bought, they have also unilaterally decided that our currency was overvalued. And like the good slave, we've devalued our naira to oblige our masters, and now we pay ten times more for what we buy from them at the same time as we receive ten times less for what we sell to them. And I understand, Sir, that the present exchange rate is only just the beginning. The devaluation has been programmed in stages, such that in few years, we shall reach the point at which we will be paying fifty, if not hundred, times more for imports and receive fifty, if not hundred, times less for our exports. Even this, they insist is still not enough. We should privatize so that their local friends and representatives could buy off what we all used to own in common. We, like the good slave again, are privatizing in full steam and are getting more hungry by the day. When we protest, as we did in May 1989, they say we are revolting and they whip us, poor slaves, back into obedience unto death. This, Sir, is SAP, and I would like to know how it is different from slavery."

"Hurrah! Hurrah!!" shouted the lecturer, loudly clapping his hands as soon as the student concluded his remarks. "That, I own, was a beautiful piece of communist propaganda. Unfortunately, it has ignored the economic causes of SAP. Since you're not interested in them and we, in any case, are not in an economics class, we shall, like you, ignore the issue and move on to more politically pertinent matters. Any more questions, the rest of you guys?" He followed his question with a theatrical opening of his arms.

"Sir, if you permit me to go back a little," a student requested, "I would like to ask a simple question."

"Go ahead, pal," the lecturer cheerfully encouraged.

"Is it not conceivable, Sir, that *perestroika* is indeed just what the Russians say it is: not the end of socialism, but a new revolution to make socialism work? And granted that this revolution may fail, as revolutions often do, it is unlikely that the failure will prevent others trying to find a different route to socialism. Don't you think, Sir, that this, in fact, is inevitable? Is it not true that as sociopolitical beings, we will forever keep trying to achieve equality even if it is ultimately impossible and no matter how often our attempts fail?"

"I think you're right," the lecturer conceded, but he quickly qualified his agreement: "You're right only to the extent that you've also affirmed that all attempts at equality are ultimately doomed to failure."

Although the class was prepared to challenge this new view, the bell announcing the end of the lecture hour sounded just then. Promising that the issue would be taken up again during the first part of the next class, the lecturer dismissed the students.

* * *

Immediately the class was over, Jagun, one of the students who had asked the most probing questions, stepped out of the lecture room and started with quickened pace to walk to the hostel.

"Jagun! Jagun!!"

He recognized the voice of Dafe, his classmate, roommate and friend. He slowed his pace.

"Where you dey hurry go?" Dafe asked as they fell in step, walking to the hostel.

"I wan touch town."

"For middle of week?"

"Bo, i rough o. I never eat since morning. My belle don dey run commentari. I wan see if my sista get sometin for pot, odawise na 0.0.0 I go take sleep dis nite."

"Me self, na *0.1.0* I still dey. Yes, i rough well, well, and *the Guy* dey tell us say SAP na to keep us for happy family of capitalism!"

"No mind am. Wetin him know? Him no get wife, no get pickin, no get relatives. How him go know say SAP hard? You no see the heavy, heavy kind jeans him dey wear, and them fine, fine chikitos him dey carry?"

"Na true, bo. Na now i good say make him dey go univacity for dis contry, no bi for Amerika where them done stuff him head full of jagbanjaitis. Any way, make I no forget: Remi say make I give you dis," and Dafe fished inside his breast pocket and brought out a handwritten note which he gave to Jagun.

"Tank you, bo," Jagun said, pocketing the note without reading it. He did this with a kind of *déjà vu* gesture which suggested he already knew or could accurately guess the content of the note.

On arriving at their room, Jagun quickly removed his shirt, trouser, and shoes, and changed into a traditional attire of *buba, soro,* and *sandals.* He bade Dafe goodbye and quickly started heading out to town.

Going to his sister for help was something Jagun never liked to do for the simple reason that she and her husband, a roadside mechanic, were in as deplorable, if not actually worse, a situation as himself. Before SAP, the sister and her husband were doing quite well. Business in the husband's car repair shed was good and she was also netting in appreciable gain from her small, wooden, and mobile front-of-the-house booth where she retailed an assortment of disparate supplies. There were household needs like sugar, tea, coffee, biscuits, and bread; smokers could purchase cigarettes and matches; school children could obtain chalk, pencil, pen, paper, eraser, and sweets; and there were toiletries like bathing soap, body lotions and pomades, combs, vanity mirrors, makeup kits, toilet paper, washing detergents, and several other items. The family was doing so well at the time that they purchased a Suzuki motor cycle, regularly sent some money home to help their parents and seriously started to save toward putting up a little bungalow in the village. Not only was it cheaper building in the village than in the city, city dwellers who came from the provinces invariably dream of eventually returning home at old age. Consequently, they see it as a necessity to build houses of their own in their towns or villages back in the regions, even as they continue to pay rents in the city. This is both a sign of success as well as a security against old age.

At the rate at which they were saving, Jagun's sister and husband had calculated that they would have put aside enough money to start work and raise their building to an appreciable level during the first year of construction, which they had tentatively planned for

1987. They lived well and their two little children were chubby, healthy, and very lively. At this time, Jagun who was still a secondary school student always looked forward to the school vacations, most of which he spent with his sister and brother-in-law in Lagos. He passed his time either playing with his niece and nephew or attending to customers who had come to purchase supplies from the mobile shop. Quite often, he would follow the brother-in-law to his mechanic's shed where he ran little errands or just loafed around. He always enjoyed these holidays, and it was in order to be close to the family that he had selected the City University of Lagos as his first choice in the national university entrance examination, JAMB.

However, by the time Jagun entered the university in October 1986, the Structural Adjustment Program (SAP) had already been put in place to deal with the economic crisis in the country. By his third year, 1989, SAP had not only proved a huge failure but had further aggravated the economic crisis. The astronomical devaluation of the naira had catapulted foreign debts and the cost of imports, drastically reduced export income, accelerated the outflow of capital, and incapacitated local industrial development. The result was a massive failure of businesses, an incredible inflation in the cost of living, mass unemployment, hunger, increased crime and political instability. The middle class practically ceased to exist, and businesses like motor repair workshops and retail provision stores, which catered to the interest of this class, went into extremely hard times.

Jagun's sister and brother-in-law and children were now ghosts of their former healthy and robust selves. The retail business had failed because they could not afford to replenish the stock in their mobile store at the new inflated prices. The brother-in-law would stay several days in his motor repair workshop without a single customer showing up. In order to survive, the motor vehicle repairer became a tire vulcanizer while his wife started selling whatever fruits were in season. She supplemented this with roasting corn, yam, or plantain for sale at the roadside near their rented one-bedroom apartment in the slums of Ajegunle to which they had recently moved from their previous two-bedroom apartment in the more decent quarters of Surulere. The first casualty was the money they had saved to build their own house in the village. The motor cycle was the next to go, followed by Jagun's sister's jewelry, china plates, party dresses, and shoes. The brother-in-law in turn sold his best clothes and, as in the case of his wife, at give-away prices. This was because each second-hand item was sold at the time the family was most desperately in need of money. Moreover, those who were buying the items were themselves just managing to survive.

Visiting his sister was now a painful experience on both sides. Jagun was unhappy seeing his sister in misery, and she in turn was sad for being unable to assist a brother in need. Going to her was thus a last resort, but Jagun preferred it to answering the call of Remi, his girlfriend and a three-hundred-level English major.

* * *

Remi, a tall black girl with the beautiful features of a model, was one of the most comfortable students on campus. She was literally bursting with money and was not averse to displaying her wealth although it was always in a manner that showed good breeding. She was always very well dressed even when she was going to lectures. Her expensive looks intimidated fellow male students, many of whom secretly envied Jagun for his "big catch." Jagun, to whom she was very generous, was very happy to help her spend the money she apparently had no good use for. She was practically his sponsor. She supplied the money with which he bought his books, paid his hostel accommodation fees, and acquired fashionable clothing. "My man must be decently dressed and at all times, you see." That was how she had boasted and she had fully backed up her boast by providing him adequate money to buy good outfits. They held the best parties in the hostel and ate at all times in the best places. Jagun knew of the hardships of SAP only from the complaints of his sister and fellow students, some of whom, like Dafe, he often treated to the leftover cash from Remi's generosity.

Jagun liked Remi a great deal. For a girl who was spoiled with money by over-rich parents, she was extremely well behaved. Although she was the one who paid the piper by settling the bills of their expenses, she allowed him to dictate the tune of their life on campus. His dream was to marry a girl who combined sophistication with respect for tradition. Remi not only possessed these attributes, but she was in addition kind, loving, quite beautiful, and from a wealthy home. What more could he want?

Jagun started making moves that would get Remi to know of his serious intention. Throughout the one year and a half he had known Remi, she had spent almost all of her weekends visiting at home in

Ibadan where her rich parents lived. A car, usually a Mercedes, a Volvo, or a 505 Peugeot would pick her up from the campus on Friday and drop her off on Sunday night. For this reason, Jagun suggested that he accompany her on one of those weekends in order to be introduced to her parents. For a long time, Remi kept putting the visit off for what seemed to Jagun to be good reasons. The first semester ended and Remi could not arrange the visit. The vacation between the semesters was ruled out because her parents had travelled to Europe and she was going directly from Lagos to join them.

The second semester began and Remi still kept postponing the visit to her parents. One weekend, she left as usual but did not return until a whole week later. Her explanation when she got back was that she had been taken ill and was briefly hospitalized in Ibadan. Apart from the fact that she did not look lean for someone who had been in a hospital, Jagun noticed she had a whole set of newly imported dresses, including a present for him consisting of a woolen pair of trousers, a lovely polo shirt, and a pair of black Italian shoes. She claimed her father had bought them at her request during a recent business trip abroad.

The coincidences made Jagun a little uneasy. The insinuating remarks of fellow students who boasted that they would rather die of SAP hardships than of AIDS caught from feasting on the leftovers of Sugar Daddy's generosity—remarks which Jagun in the past had dismissed as mere invidious statements provoked by envy—now started to sound bothersome. Jagun began developing suspicion when a student openly boasted and apparently for his benefit, that while they might survive the plague of SAP, death or life prison terms inescapably awaited cocaine dealers and their accomplices.

Jagun's peace of mind was completely shattered when later he suddenly discovered a page, torn from *NA-SO-I-BE*, the students' weekly cartoon magazine, secretly tucked by someone into the pages of one of his lecture note books. The cartoon depicted a row of university girls including some who had already graduated, lined up in front of a super luxurious hotel, located in some unnamed capital city that could be Lagos, Lisbon, London, New York, Paris, or Rome. Emerging from the hotel was a particularly gorgeous, tall black student from whose overloaded pockets and bags excess currencies from various foreign countries were falling in generous quantities.

In another corner of the same cartoon, there was a depiction of the contrasting scene of a crumbling university campus with famished, haggard-looking students, clutching emptiness where there ought to have been books. One of the scarecrow figures representing students was highlighted, thinking: *"Bo, before SAP send me go da kingdom, make man pickin go find original chikito like that one wey dey swim for money!"* The thinker's hand was drawn pointing to the gorgeous, tall black girl as she emerges from the hotel. Continuing his day-dreaming, the scarecrow thinker philosophically weighs the options: *"After all, SAP dey kill fasta dan AIDS. Any ways, i fit be say Oyinbo witch go find cure for AIDS before man go quench!"*

Looking at the cartoon, Jagun started to sweat profusely. He was confused and scared as if he were actually confronted with incontrovertible evidence rather than mere suspicions. He emerged from the mood of confusion and fear into that of determination, though underlined with anxiety, to find out at all costs if the cartoon had anything to do with Remi.

Not long after this incident, Jagun went one evening to see Remi but found her door locked and a note, left for her by an earlier caller, stuck to the door. It was a Thursday and the note had instructed her to collect her tickets the next day at the International airport counter of Swissair at least an hour before departure. The writer of the note profusely apologized for breaking her injunction forbidding him leaving her notes. He explained that he had no alternative since earlier arrangements had changed and he had to go overseas immediately. Jagun reread the note in disbelief because, earlier in the week, Remi had already told him that she would be going home to Ibadan as usual that weekend and that she was not likely to return till midweek because the doctor who had treated her when she was sick the previous month had asked her to return for a check-up.

Jagun's first reaction, reading the note that confirmed his worst suspicion, was the sharp pains of extreme disappointment. Then a sudden unaccountable weight resulting from an overwhelming weakness began to press him down. He broke into a sudden profuse sweat that threatened to drown him, and he started to shake with fear as it dawned on him that he was perhaps already an AIDS carrier. He felt as if he were sinking gradually to the ground, but he summoned all his will power to pull himself together and move away from the scene. He walked blindly back to his hostel and flopped on his bed.

When Remi returned on the Wednesday of the following week, she went to look for Jagun and, not finding him, left him a note which said: "Jagun, I can't wait to see you. It's been like an age. Come and see me: I have a surprise for you." It was signed: "Your darling, Remi."

* * *

When Jagun got to his sister's, he suspected immediately that something was wrong. Her mobile booth was locked up and she was not roasting food to sell at the usual place. This was unfortunate for he had planned immediately on arrival to grab whatever she might have been roasting—yam, plantain, or corn—and devour his hunger away. As soon as he entered the apartment and also saw that his brother-in-law was at home rather than at work, he knew that something was definitely wrong. Both his sister and her husband were sitting with downcast heads, hands folded on their laps, looking resigned and defeated.

"What's the matter?" Jagun asked, his unexpected voice jerking the couple awake from their bitter reverie. They both suddenly looked up with a momentary flash of hope going across their faces which soon returned to the former defeated look of resignation when they saw it was only Jagun.

"Doja has been sick and getting worse by the day for over a week," the brother-in-law huskily said.

"Have you been to see a doctor?"

"We have, but could not find money to pay the compulsory deposit for admission."

"Didn't they give you any prescription?"

"They did."

"And so?"

"We spent our last kobo paying the bus fare to the hospital and the pharmacist refused to sell on credit. The friends we contacted told us what we know to be true: that they themselves were barely managing to survive SAP from day to day and that they had no money to loan us. I stayed at the repair workshop daily until today and no customers came. Our last hope is my brother who works as a messenger in the Ministry of Education. He said before the end of the day he must find someone to loan him something. He took the prescription along with him. Actually, we though he was the one who had arrived when you came in."

Jagun walked over to the bed where the sick child was lying. Her body was extremely hot to his touch and she was incredibly emaciated. The little girl who used to be so happy to see him could not even recognize him. His eyes misted, but he knew he must control his emotions or else his sister and brother-in-law who, judging from the huskiness of the latter's voice, must have already cried their hearts out, might begin again. Instead, he directed a question at his sister who had not spoken a word since he arrived. He enquired after Jegede, her first child, a boy.

"We sent him home with a friend to Mama last week when we could no longer feed him," she answered. Her barely audible voice was dry and husky, evidently from grief and too much crying. "Jagun," she then called, "do you not have anything on you, even your food money?"

"Nothing," Jagun replied after a brief silence. "I actually came here, hoping to find something to eat."

"Your girlfriend must have dumped you then. I thought you were not looking well yourself. We have about some five milk cups of *garri* left in the house. Go and soak some in water to eat. There is no soup to make *eba.*"

"Somehow," Jagun replied, "I'm just not hungry any more."

"Because you want to spare the *garri?*" the brother-in-law asked in a mixed tone of sadness and loving accusation.

"No, honestly I no longer feel hungry," he affirmed, and it was true that the sharp hunger he had felt earlier had mysteriously disappeared.

When Jagun returned later to the hostel that evening, Dafe knew without being told that his friend's trip to the sister had been fruitless and that Jagun had not yet eaten anything all day. He went quietly out of the room to the kiosk in their common room and bought a small loaf of bread. This meant that he too would come a day sooner than anticipated to the "triple zero," no-food situation being presently experienced by Jagun, but he did not mind. He returned to their room and without a word handed over the bread in its brown packet to Jagun. The latter instantly recognized the content of the parcel by its smell. He was overwhelmed with gratitude and he thanked Dafe who simply remarked: "Na we go bury SAP, no bi him go bury us."

In the morning, Jagun announced to Dafe's dismay that he was not going to attend classes but going home to find means of surviving the remaining weeks of the semester.

"How you go manage for transport?" Dafe asked.

"I go hitch-hike."

"For now, when some dey take even dem own pickin make medicine for money! Bo, i dangerous well, well; make you no try am at all."

"Make you no worry. I go dey fine. And when you see Remi, tell am say I go see am when I return."

* * *

The political lecture on *perestroika* marked the sixth day after Jagun had an interview with Remi since the accidental discovery of the note on her door and since her mid-week return from overseas, following which she had sent Jagun a love note of invitation which he had ignored. She was surprised that Jagun did not answer her call that evening, nor the next day, or the day after. When a few more days passed and Jagun still had not come to see her, despite sending additional frantic notes of invitation, it became obvious to Remi that Jagun would not on his own come to her. It was then that she took matters into her own hands because she genuinely missed him and badly wanted to see him and could no longer bear to be separated from him any longer. She checked his class schedule and went to wait for him just as he was leaving lecture.

Jagun's first impulse on seeing Remi was to walk away, but he changed his mind because he did not want to create a scene before his classmates. So he allowed her to fall in step, but he selected the longer and less-frequented route back to the hostel in order to avoid his coursemates.

"Jagun, why have you been torturing me by not answering my calls?" Her tone was a mixture of heart-felt hurt and deep anxiety.

"What do you want with me? When will you stop pretending? Did it not occur to you that I have found you out?" There was silence.

"You saw the note then— the one left on my door about airplane tickets." She said this in a tone of affirmation rather than of question. Her voice was barely audible. The realization that what she had feared the most had happened made her extremely weak and helpless. "I guessed as much," she added. Her voice was full of self-pity.

"Did you think I would never know? And if you loved me as much as you claimed you did, why didn't you think twice before exposing me to public ridicule and the mortal danger of AIDS?"

"Who said you've been exposed to AIDS?" she quickly asked with alarm and concern.

"Who knows how many different men you junket with to the world capitals every weekend, and how many times over you've contacted the virus!" He said this in a tone of certainty and regrets than as a question.

"Well," she replied, heaving a great sigh of relief, "if this is your only source of fear, then you can relax. I do not junket with several men and I do not have any disease."

"What else would you have said? In any case, how would you know?"

His tone was derisive. She recognized the derision and was hurt, but she ignored it. Rather, in a tone of absolute certainty, leaving no room for any atom of doubt, she said simply:

"I know."

In spite of himself, Jagun felt a great relief. For the first time since he developed suspicions, he started admitting the possibility that he might have rashly jumped to conclusions and that he might not have contacted the dreadful disease. The embarrassing silence that followed was broken by Remi who was silently heaving in a muffled crying and periodically wiping tears with an handkerchief.

"I know how dreadfully disappointed you must be, Jagun. You might also have been wondering why I got myself into this mess. I know you may not be interested, but I would like to tell you. I want you to know because I deeply love you. Wherever I go, or whatever I do, I constantly think of you because you're the only one I love. I like to hope that after hearing me, you might understand and possibly forgive me."

She was silent for a while as she quietly wiped her tears. She looked completely defeated and pitiable.

"By the time I got admitted to the University, my parents had been completely wiped out by SAP. The same SAP made it impossible for me, or any secondary school leaver for that matter, to obtain employment. The alternatives before me were either to get myself married to some fool who would treat me shabbily or to start endlessly roaming the streets, hopelessly searching for work that was certainly not there and surviving on handouts and prostitution. I decided I must find my way to the University both for my own sake and in order not to remain a burden on my parents."

Remi stopped briefly to observe if Jagun was listening and how he was listening. She was encouraged by what she saw and she continued after first wiping her tears.

"I tried the local, state, and federal government scholarship boards without luck. The boards too were a casualty to SAP, with little or no allocations from the governments. The same was true of the loan boards. It was at this point that I ran into this man at a party. He said he was a multimillionaire and that he would do for me anything money could handle. He was good-looking, in his early fifties, well kept, chairman/managing director of one of those new Banks which sprang up in the wake of SAP. I saw it as my only way out even if it was not honorable. He has treated me well, been very generous, and respected my wish not to imperil my health or my future."

She was silent for a moment while she wiped her tears, stole a look at Jagun before proceeding in a quieter tone.

"He knows I deeply love you and has often reminded me to find something decent for you during our travels, as if I needed his urging. That is his way of getting on my good side. He is conscious of the fact that my relationship with him is forced and he does his best to make it less painful. But it has remained painful because I have always been uneasy, afraid you would sooner or later know the truth and that I would lose you."

She stopped, and again an embarrassing silence followed because she was expecting Jagun to say something. Although he didn't say anything, she observed that the expression on his face was a little more sympathetic than before.

"That's my story," she stated to elicit his response. "I know you must be badly disappointed but I want you to know that I honestly, most truly love you. I will do anything to atone for my sins and retain your love. I'm fairly comfortable now and beyond the immediate reach of SAP. I can stop seeing him right now if you say so."

After a long silence, Jagun finally made a reply, which though noncommittal was sufficiently reassuring to Remi who had feared the worst.

"All this is too much for me to swallow right now. I need time to think about it. But whatever happens, I want you to know that I deeply appreciate your saving me from becoming an early casualty to SAP. Without your support, I would have dropped out since last year. You should know too, that I cared an awful lot about you. Probably that was why I remained blind for this long, dismissing offhand the loud insinuations of fellow students. It is, you see, going to be emotionally hard for me, too. And doubly hard as well because I'm still within the stranglehold of SAP. But I need time to think about it."

Having said this, Jagun quickened his pace to go away without any formal words of parting. The old fear that this might be the last time she would see or speak with Jagun suddenly gripped Remi again. Her heart sank out of fear, tears gushed from her eyes as she struggled with her sobs to plead with him.

"Jagun," she sobbingly called; and when he had looked back, she added quickly: "Please, remember, I love you. I do dearly love you." There was desperation in her weak, crying, and pleading voice.

In spite of Jagun's noncommittal response to her plea for the continuation of their relationship, Remi had hoped that he would be moved by his love for her to return to her within days. She was certain he would return soon to her because she could not think of her life without him. She daily expected him to knock on her door, but the first and second days passed and there was no knock. After the third day and there was still no sign of him, Remi started losing hope, but she refused to give up. On the fourth and fifth day, she had sent a brief note to let him know how much she loved and missed him. The note from her on the sixth day which Dafe delivered after the *perestroika* lecture was still in Jagun's pocket as he rode the bus to town in order to find something to eat at his sister's. When he finally took out the note, unfolded and read it, the message was brief and simple: "I'm miserable without you," it said.

* * *

On the third day of seriously pondering over the matter, Jagun decided there was nothing to forgive Remi for and that she was as much a victim of SAP as he himself. He admitted in his mind that he still loved her and he also knew that she loved him. He would have gone directly back to her embrace but, having now known the source of her money, and having decided not to accept any further support from her, he knew it would be impossible to establish a decent relationship until he was financially independent. He knew too that it would take time, but he equally believed that if their love was genuine, it could wait. The wait should enable them to sort out their true feelings for each other and allow them to discover if the present deep attachments and pains of separation were only passing emotions that would soon be lost and forgotten without regrets. This was what he had decided to tell her at the appropriate time after returning from the visit home.

Although Jagun took a lot of beating from the intense heat of the sun while waiting for free rides, he was able to hitch-hike home without any incident. Even though he had arrived very late at night instead of the early evening which was the usual arrival time by paid transportation, he was glad he made it home safely. The experience, by and large, was in fact good. Once the vehicle owners had assured themselves that they had not in error picked a disguised armed robber, they were usually nice. And generous too in sharing their drinks and snacks.

His parents were disturbed to see him, thinking he had brought bad news concerning his sister's family. They were visibly relieved to know that Doja, their granddaughter, was still battling to live even though he bluntly told them he doubted she could survive. Their worry returned when he told them that he had come because he had been starving.

"Well, the village is no longer the place to come to alleviate city hunger, my son," the father said.

"My mother will turn in her grave to learn that we in this village now starve for food," the mother added.

"We now get better prices in the market for the food we grow, but those people who brought this thing called SAP are cunning people. They knew well what they were doing. We now pay several times more for the things we must buy; consequently, we have to sell so much more than we did in the past. The result is that we don't have enough food left to eat nor can we afford the things we used to be able to buy. I have sold everything I have for selling this season, yet, unlike in the past, I have not been able to pay all of this term's school fees for your brother and sister. And another thing, the land is exhausted and cannot yield as before despite all the expensive fertilizers we put in."

"Dad," Jagun said, "I know all of these things that you're telling me, and that is why you haven't seen me here earlier. Now my situation has reached the crisis point, and I have to dropout, unless I can find the money to feed for the rest of the semester. But I must not dropout, so we must find the money, even if it is in the devil's own nest."

"Very rough, I see," the father said.

"I think we should all go to sleep," the mother advised. "Please God and our ancestors, we'll wake up in the morning with the wisdom to know what to do."

"I think your mother is right, son."

They bade good night and retired. In the morning, the family decided that since there were no personal resources to tap for money, there was no alternative to borrowing. A list of those to be approached, who among them to make the approach, and at what time, was drawn up. They hoped to raise enough to send some help to Jagun's sister in Lagos, pay the school fees of Jagun's younger brother and sister, and provide the needs of Jagun himself. The parents and Jagun would reassemble in the night to compare notes.

When they did, the results were very disappointing. Nobody succeeded in raising any loan. The stories were the same everywhere they went. Many were yet to pay their own children's school fees and the houses they were building had been abandoned; evidences were produced of obligations which could not be met; letters from sons, daughters and close relations in colleges, universities, and various cities, seeking financial and material assistance which could not be rendered were also presented. Those they had expected to be comfortable turned out to be heavily indebted and were just managing to meet Bank monthly payments.

Since the door seemed closed on personal loans, the family resolved to try bank loans. In the morning of the second day of their search, they went to the town which was an hour's journey from the village. They were turned away by the biggest of the two banks in the town because they had no account there. In the second smaller bank, which was more receptive, they discovered that their village house could not be used as collateral as it had no legal documents and experience had shown that to procure the necessary documents, more than a year was required. The only loan they could have qualified for was agricultural loan, but this was not an agricultural matter and, in any case, it would require at least three months to process. The family returned to the village in disappointment.

The only option now left was for them to wait till Sunday and try out the community age-group meetings. Jagun spent the intervening day which was a Saturday with his father, looking over the farm which in another month would be cultivated. They trimmed the shoots of seed yams that were germinating too early, and returned home. On Sunday, it turned out that some unions would grant loans only to members. Those that would have bent the rules because of the serious circumstances the family was in, complained they had no money because their members were not paying dues or repaying loans. They explained that apart from the fact that SAP had stripped

everybody dry, it was an off-season period for farmers and, consequently, it was the worst time for anyone to ask for a loan. Refusing
to be defeated, Jagun's parents went back to try the personal loan
strategy, visiting this time those they had not asked the first day. At
the end of the day, all they got as loan was just enough to pay for
Jagun's transport back to the university.

Jagun, of course, decided to save the money and return by the
same way he had come—hitch-hiking. He would give the money to
his sister for drugs if his sick niece was still alive. He would similarly
give her the food the mother had asked him to share with her.
Strangely enough, he was not depressed. The failure to raise money
at home had only made him more resolute. He believed that there
must be a way out of his predicament and he was determined to find
it. Since relatives were unable to help, there ought to be some stranger
somewhere in Lagos who would help. And he would find this
stranger, he decided. He refused to contemplate even for a second the
possibility that he might eventually be forced to join the dropouts
who, from peddling drugs in the international markets were either in
prison or swimming in money, or those in the underworld of crime,
doing armed robbery, car-snatching, burglary, and petty stealing. He
prayed he would never become that desperate.

* * *

Jagun waited patiently on the roadside waving down cars going
to Lagos for a free ride. He waited a long time. Some drivers zoomed
past without a thought. Some hesitated, slowed down, looked at him,
changed their minds and accelerated again. Jagun was not bitter,
knowing that if he were a car owner himself, he too would be wary
of giving lifts to strangers in this era of SAP when even a friend could
snatch a friend's car. He waited patiently on the roadside, buoyed by
the optimism that he would sooner or later find a ride.

His optimism paid off because after a long while a car stopped.
To his pleasant surprise, the driver turned out to be his former
Chemistry teacher at the secondary school. It was because the former
teacher had recognized Jagun who was his best student that he had
stopped. The former Chemistry teacher was now a medical doctor on
his annual leave from Saudi Arabia where he was now practicing, having, like many, been made to flee there by SAP. He was disappointed
that Jagun had not chosen to study medicine, but he was intrigued

by his former student's argument which claimed that Nigeria needed good politicians more than she needed doctors at that particular time.

"If we have the right leadership," Jagun said, "we will train as many doctors as we need. Doctors like you will not be abroad when there is a chronic shortage of doctors in the country. Brilliant students will not be compelled to dropout of colleges and universities and be driven by desperation into becoming prostitutes, cocaine dealers, armed robbers, street beggars, mad people, or suicide cases. So you see, Sir, good politicians will be savers of life—doctors in their own right."

"Yes, Jagun, your answer is right as usual, absolutely right. But tell me how you're doing, how you're coping with SAP, how you're finding university life, what it is like studying politics."

Jagun could not resist telling him about his hardships. "And there is no certainty that even if I overcome these problems and earn a good degree, I will find a job at the end of the day. But I'm determined that nothing will stop me from becoming an important political decision maker in this country. There are millions of my generation who are equally determined to transform this country, this present junkyard of capitalism, into a respected and self-respecting nation that can clothe, feed, and protect its citizens. SAP, just like slavery and colonialism, will end. Only, this time, we will ensure that it is not merely replaced by another more sophisticated form of oppression."

Jagun had spoken throughout calmly, without heat, a fact that had further accentuated the gravity of what he said. The doctor was deeply impressed by the contrast between Jagun's optimism and the depressing situation he was actually in.

"And you say, you yet have no idea where you'll get help in Lagos?" the doctor asked Jagun.

"It's true. I don't know but I must find it. I have no other option since I do not want to push drugs or join the underworld," Jagun replied.

"Hm," the doctor grunted. "I must say I admire your spirit. But let's see if we can change to a more pleasant topic of discussion."

Jagun had no objection to changing the topic. However, anything they discussed as they sped along bumpy roads to Lagos had a way of bringing them back in spite of themselves to the depressing reality of the country. On arriving in Lagos, the doctor dropped Jagun off at Jagun's sister's apartment. Jagun thanked him profusely and was about to go when the doctor gave him a visiting card.

"Well, about your problem," the doctor casually began, "I think I know someone who would be glad to help you without undermining your pride or integrity. Come and see me at that address at ten in the morning tomorrow."

The doctor bade good night and drove away, happy in the anticipation of personally contributing to the making of what promises to be a better tomorrow.

———————————